SPY
ON THE RUN

By Marc Lovell

SPY ON THE RUN
THE SPY WITH HIS HEAD IN THE CLOUDS
THE SPY GAME
HAND OVER MIND
A VOICE FROM THE LIVING
THE SECOND VANETTI AFFAIR
THE BLIND HYPNOTIST
DREAMERS IN A HAUNTED HOUSE
AN ENQUIRY INTO THE EXISTENCE OF VAMPIRES
A PRESENCE IN THE HOUSE
THE IMITATION THIEVES
THE GHOST OF MEGAN

SPY
ON THE RUN

MARC LOVELL

PUBLISHED FOR THE CRIME CLUB BY
DOUBLEDAY & COMPANY, INC.
GARDEN CITY, NEW YORK
1982

All of the characters in this book
are fictitious, and any resemblance
to actual persons, living or dead,
is purely coincidental.

Library of Congress Cataloging in Publication Data

Lovell, Marc.
Spy on the run.

I. Title.
PR6062.0853S694   1982   823
ISBN 0-385-18095-0   AACR2

Library of Congress Catalog Card Number 81-43778
Copyright © 1982 by Doubleday & Company, Inc.
All Rights Reserved
Printed in the United States of America
First Edition

SPY
ON THE RUN

CHAPTER 1

Appleton Porter went into Kensington Gardens, which spreads its green and pretty self from the glamour of Kensington to the glum of Bayswater, like a decent suit between a fresh shave and shabby shoes.

He walked at a stroll. His hands were clasped loosely behind him. No one, he assured himself, would guess how he was feeling.

Apple was excited.

Children were making oompah sounds on the bandstand, pretending to be musicians. A drunk and his bottle lay emptily on the grass. Against a tree, a young couple necked as violently as if it were midnight, instead of after five on a summer afternoon. A scattering of people wandered casually, either on the grass or on the same broad tarmac path that Apple was using.

There were nannies with prams that looked as if they had been made by Rolls-Royce. Over by the pond, men were radio-controlling their miniature ocean liners and yachts, watched by small boys whose envy was hidden behind sneers.

But Appleton Porter was neither seeing nor thinking about his surroundings. Normally he would be reminding himself that the London Museum, on his left, was, as Kensington Palace, the birthplace of Queen Victoria, and that the exhibits had been moved there in 1951 from Lancaster House, former home of that famous grand old Duke of York.

Apple had a fondness for irrelevant detail and useless facts.

His most recent addition to his store was that a human being uses 70 percent of his energy merely in keeping himself upright. Apple had wondered about that; wondered if someone of his own size needed to use more, say 80 percent. But he hadn't fretted over it too much. Apple was only mildly neurotic, much less than the norm, which sometimes worried him.

Appleton Porter was six feet seven inches tall. What made that worse was him being thin with it—though not to the point of skinniness: there was muscular flesh on his long bones.

Apple had sandy hair cut to Establishment neatness. His skin was pale where it spread free of the tawny freckles. Like a model for your average middle-class Englishman, his face was unremarkable but acceptably good-looking—straight nose, mouth of little sensuality, square chin. His best feature was the keen green eyes.

As always when anywhere except at home, Apple was neatly turned out. He wore a white shirt, a morose tie of subdued, timid checks, and a dark suit that had stripes which, unusually, went across instead of down. This horizontal formation, Apple felt, tended to lessen the height and disguise his thinness.

He no more liked being six feet seven inches tall than he did his build or his colouring or the freckles that disappeared only when he blushed. But there was nothing he could do about any of these self-assumed frailties, so he told himself there was no point in worrying about it. He told himself every other day.

Now, this sunny afternoon, Apple was thinking only of what lay ahead. He hardly noticed when a passer-by glanced up at him with an expression of whimsy. He was musing that it could turn out to be something big. Really big. It made no difference that he didn't really believe this. He went on musing bigness.

Apple was excited.

He dawdled to a halt. From his inside breast pocket he brought out a packet of cigarettes. He used his left hand to put a cigarette between his lips—and during the act took a quick, sly glance at his wristwatch, as if it belonged to somebody else.

There were eight minutes left to go, he saw. He would be there on the dot.

An hour earlier, the telephone had rung in his office at the United Kingdom Philological Institute, where Apple was a senior official. The caller was Angus Watkin, although he didn't give his name, simply stating a number. Even without that, Apple would have recognised the dull, damp, bored-sounding voice.

"Are you alone, Porter?" Watkin asked.

"Yes, sir, and I can't be overheard." He assumed that the line was clean, on scrambler at the other end.

"I shall give you your instructions one time only. You will then repeat them back to me. Understood?"

"Perfectly, sir," Apple said. He was sitting bolt upright with anticipation. "I know the routine."

"One would hope so," Angus Watkin said. "But to the matter. Which is as follows: This afternoon you will cross Kensington Gardens at a time that will get you to the Bayswater Road at quarter past five. On the opposite side of the road you will see a yellow car. It will be parked with its nearside wheels on the kerb. The one passenger, the driver, will be wearing a grey hat. Am I going too fast for you?"

Although he knew that Watkin would have been pleased with an answer in the affirmative, and although he wanted to please Watkin, Apple nevertheless said:

3

"No, sir, that's fine." A greater want was to seem sharp, alert. In any case, Angus Watkin wasn't speaking at much more than normal speed. Not unusually, there had been a tinge of sarcasm in his voice when he had asked the question.

He went on, "You will go over to the car and tell its driver that he is illegally parked. He will answer that it is none of your business. You will then say, quote, 'I shall report you to the police, Mr. Jones,' unquote. He will say, quote, 'Please do that, Mr. Smith,' unquote. You will then open the rear door and get in. Those are your instructions. Give them back to me, please."

When he had finished the repeat, verbatim in respect of the exchange of signals, Apple asked, following a slight pause, "And then what, sir?"

"Stage Two you will get from the driver, Porter," Angus Watkin said. "Good afternoon." The line went dead.

Now, Apple got out his lighter and put flame to his cigarette. He drew hungrily at the smoke. Stage Two, he thought. It meant that this was no simple matter. It was not a drop or a pick-up. He had no message to deliver, nothing to collect. He wasn't playing courier. It had to be something big. Big and worthwhile. Important.

Urgently, Apple brought his hand to his mouth. His lips felt nothing but fingers. Looking down at the ground, he saw that he had dropped the cigarette and squashed it out underfoot.

Apple was excited.

Afting his hands again, keeping the clasp loose, he strolled on. He thought: Seven minutes to go until rendezvous time. You are calm. You are cool. You are so collected it isn't true.

Apple's nerves clanged and his body gave a mammoth jerk when the woman screamed.

The scream had come from somewhere behind him. He swung around fast. For some odd reason his eyes went first to the rooftops of Kensington, to the flagless flagpole that topped the building which housed the United Kingdom Philological Institute. Next, he shortened his vision.

As Apple saw the woman, she screamed again. This time the sound was formed around a word: "Stop." She was standing side-on, her arms raised. Before following with his eyes the direction of those arms, Apple had time only to note that the woman was young and wearing a fawn dress.

A man was running away across the grass. He held a brown leather bag which had a long shoulder strap.

"Help!" the woman screamed. "Thief!"

Apple burst into action. Behind it lay no thought, no order to respond. He was moved by instinct. In two flying strides he had left the path. He ran at full speed after the bag-snatcher.

The man was ten yards ahead. He wore shirt and jeans of denim, white sneakers turned grey with age. His hair was blond and cropped almost to a stubble.

A Skinhead, Apple thought.

The woman had stopped screaming, though there were unintelligible shouts coming from behind.

In front, beyond the bag-snatcher, an old man made a try at interference. He stood with arms and legs spread, as if guarding a goal. The blond dodged him easily and ran on in the same direction. There was no one else ahead.

Apple ran furiously. He had closed the gap to eight yards. His chin was thrust far out with determination, his long legs were stretching to their limits in huge strides, his arms were wheeling. He felt confident of success.

The bag-snatcher glanced back. He looked too old to be a member of the teenage trouble-loving cultists called Skinheads. He was somewhere in his early twenties. His face was plump and had a corrupt expression. He was average height.

And I am not, Apple thought. I'll catch you, you thieving sod. I'm gaining by the second.

The gap was down to six or seven yards. In his growing confidence, Apple looked behind. The only person to have joined in the chase was the woman. She, Apple saw with admiration, was coming along at a good speed.

When Apple faced front again, his admiration went grudgingly to the thief. In order to allow freedom to both arms, he had put the shoulder strap over his head. The man was a pro.

Apple ran hard. His body was reacting well, but already his lungs were beginning to feel the effect of twenty cigarettes a day. And he noticed that the gap was staying at six yards. He had stopped gaining.

Despite the comparative shortness of his legs, the thief was keeping ahead, with the leather bag floating out behind.

Apple flailed his legs and arms. His mouth was wide open for air. To help in the action, he started to rock his head from side to side and, more usefully, told himself that he was Roger Bannister, during the breaking of the four-minute barrier in the mile, at Oxford on May 6, 1954.

The blond man ahead seemed to be running with the greatest of ease. There was no panic in his movements. To Apple, his lungs now paining, there was an aspect about the picture that was sadly strange.

He took a quick glance back. The woman was still coming. Behind her, no one else looked to be involved.

Turning front, Apple gave everything he had to the chase. He ran, ran, ran. His head rocked, his limbs circled, his feet stabbed the ground rapidly.

The next minute, he got a surge of delight. It came from seeing that the gap was shrinking quickly. It was not, he noted, due to his own efforts, but because the bag-snatcher was slowing.

The blond slowed further still, circled to the left so that he was back facing the way he had come, and, unlooping the strap from his head, tossed the bag away. It landed on the grass directly in Apple's path.

Then the man sat down.

Apple went on over the bag as he reduced speed. Unsteadily, he came to a halt. He drooped, gasping. To help his lungs he put both hands to his rear hips. He turned and started to walk back.

With dull shock, Apple saw that the blond was smiling. He swung the smile from Apple toward the woman, who was slowing from her run. She returned the smile as she moved toward the blond. When near him, she stopped and also sat on the grass. The pair of them sat hugging their knees and seemed to be not too badly out of breath.

Apple arrived opposite the pair, beside the bag. He was panting heavily, still not able to straighten from his stoop. Looking from smiling man to smiling woman he thought, Christ. A couple of idiots. They're together in this. It's nothing more than a game they play for some childish, moronic reason of their own. And I fell for it.

Tiredly furious, Apple bent down and picked up the bag. Lifting its flap, he looked inside—at emptiness. That, he realised, had been what had appeared strange about the picture of the running man ahead. A full bag would have bounced, not floated out behind. He was stupid not to have realised that.

Apple, throwing the bag aside, said in a controlled voice, "Listen to me, you pair of bloody . . ."

He didn't finish. He forgot his fury. He had remembered the rendezvous on Bayswater Road.

Apple snatched a look at his watch. It showed that he had less than three minutes left. It wasn't enough. Even if he ran like a demon he would be late. The operation could well be over before it had got started.

Straightening with a huge intake of air, Apple swung his upper body backwards in preparation to take off at a flying run. He held himself there, frozen, when the blond man said, "Forget it, Porter."

Apple blinked slowly, slowly. As he eased his trunk forward out of the leaning pose, he began to blush.

Appleton Porter had worked for British Intelligence since leaving university, where he had been a star in Modern Languages. His don, Professor Green, recruited him after Apple had been tentatively approached by another don, Atwater. Professor Atwater, Apple learned, was a Communist. He recruited for the other side.

Apple had been eager to join. He had then had, and retained still, a romantic attitude toward the sub-world of espionage: the cloak of darkness, the dagger that hisses through the air. He was an avid reader of spy fiction. He used the spook slang: Mayflower for American, Hammer for a male KGB agent and Sickle for a female, Upstairs for the higher reaches of the British secret services. He preferred the James Bond type of movie.

Having happily agreed to become a player in the spy game, Apple had been faced with only one decision. Professor Green had said, "If you wish, we can let Atwater hook you. In which case, you would become, of course, a double agent. The choice is yours—doubling or singling."

Fearing that he might find the two-faced image beyond his ability, Apple had opted to play it straight. He had been regretting that decision ever since. As a double, he often thought morosely, he at least would have seen some action once in a while.

In all his years of service, Apple had been out in the field as an agent only twice. His chief contribution to Intelligence was connected with languages—his position at the United Kingdom

Philological Institute was both a cover and a legitimate occupation: he got paid as a civil servant as well as receiving an ample retainer from Intelligence.

Apple spoke six languages with perfect fluency, another five with competence but a noticeable accent, and had a sound knowledge of seven more. Philology was his love and his labour. He was presently studying the world's number óne mystery language—Basque.

For MI5 and MI6, occasionally for the Special Branch, Apple did translations, checked decoded messages for verbal ambiguities, sat in as interpreter on high-level conferences when Western secret service people were pretending to trust one another. The work had its points of interest, but could hardly be called exciting.

Apple numbered among the faceless ones in Intelligence. These were the employees with specialities which ranged from picking pockets to weight-lifting, reading the finger-language of mutes to the ability to self-dislocate a joint; specialities that might be needed only once a year or once in a career.

Apple knew why he wasn't used more often, even as a lowly courier. It had nothing to do with his ratings after his period of training at Damian House and other, less attractive places. It wasn't because he had scored only five out of ten for resistance to physical pain (though making nine in the mental variety). It wasn't because he had earned a lowly six for inventiveness in lying. And it certainly wasn't because of the five he got in tolerance for alcohol.

His lack of activity was on account of what came under the heading of Remarks on the back of his dossier.

Apple knew that dossier word for word. He had sweet-talked a secretary from Upstairs into smuggling out to him a photocopy, which he had burned after mentally devouring—burned with a beautiful spy-like feeling.

9

Appleton Porter was too tall for successful dimming of presence, Remarks said, the vital need to become one of the herd. Furthermore, Appleton Porter had a sympathetic nature, which would be a drawback if a mission called for ruthlessness. Appleton Porter was also given to blushing.

To hide his scorching face, Apple turned away from the couple who were sitting on the grass. He fought back against the blush with the method he was currently using, latest in a long line, for each soon became useless due to familiarity.

Apple had always before bought these anti-blush methods through advertisements in magazines. The newest he had found in a newspaper's agony column. Aunt Maud told Often Crimson that to cure an attack she should imagine that an evil-looking man was bringing a blowtorch close to her face; fear and the idea of super heat would quickly send the blush into retreat.

Apple tried. Closing his eyes, he conjured up the man, whose face was grotesque, and saw the flaring torch. But the picture began to flicker. Apple couldn't concentrate.

He was telling himself grimly that, of course, there was no yellow car on Bayswater Road, parked illegally or otherwise. There was no man in a grey hat. There would be no one waiting to exchange signals with. There would be no Stage Two.

Apple opened his eyes. He gazed up at the sky. His grimness faded, and he realised that his blush had faded also, without any help from his imagination. He was beginning to understand that this could only mean a Stage One. Something was happening. The elaborate set-up had not been arranged for fun.

The pair behind were talking. Apple tuned in. The man said, "I'd put it at three thousand myself."

"Sure," the woman said. "Those long stems." Her accent was that of an American.

"The five, I think, is out of the question." He was definitely British. "You have to consider the lasting quality."

"Which you'd need less of for the three, natch. So it's now a matter of technique."

The man said, "I might mention that you're rather nifty in that department yourself."

"You're not exactly a beginner, either."

"May I ask your name, by the way?"

"Don't see why not," the girl said. "Call me June."

"I'm Philip. Hello."

"Hello, Philip."

Apple turned. The pair glanced at him, then looked back at each other. The girl who had given herself the name of June said, "It's not going to be easy. Did you see the action?"

"Not much. A glance or two. It seemed decent enough."

"There was the juvenile head-wagging bit. That has to go. But really go."

"Christ, yes. Maybe he's a five after all."

June said, "No, Philip, I'd swear he's a three. And listen, I've seen plenty."

They went on talking, using numbers and figures. It was all over Apple's head. Not that he was paying particular attention. He was having a good, close look at June.

She was a year or two younger than his own age—twenty-eight. Her face was prettier than average, helped by a suntan. She had dimples, gleaming teeth, an upturned nose. Her eyes were large and dark, the same deep brown as her hair, which was short and curly like a cap of bubbles. She had an earnest expression.

June was still sitting with her legs bent up. The hem of her dress barely covered her knees. From his angle, Apple could see a sliver of under-thigh. He thought that if he moved to the left a little . . .

What a dirty bastard you are, he told himself. Thank God.

Apple began to move—to the left. The man and woman broke off their talk. June looked over while casually sending her legs down straight and neatening her dress.

Apple stopped. He smiled at her and said, "Hello."

June looked at him carefully. After giving a slow nod, she smiled back. "Hi. How's the breathing?"

"Fine now, thank you." I'm smitten, he thought.

The man called Philip said, "Good afternoon, sir."

Apple shot him a startled look. "Eh?"

Philip was getting up while looking at Apple. June had started to do the same. She said, "Good afternoon, sir."

It now came to Apple that the two were not looking *at* him, but behind him. He turned. He said, "Good afternoon, sir."

"Hello, Porter," Angus Watkin said, almost wearily, as if they had met three times already today, whereas Apple had not seen the man in months.

Watkin was leaning against the trunk of a nearby tree, which he gave the impression of having rented for the season. His age was in the mid-fifties. He seemed to be mid-everything. There was nothing at all about him out of the ordinary. His face was bland, forgettable. The sleepy eyes gave no hint of sharpness, no suggestion of intelligence beyond the norm. His brow wasn't high. His mouth looked soft, not cruel or determined. His hair was neat without being strict.

Wearing a fawn, plain, summerweight raincoat, Angus Watkin would never have to strive to become one of the herd. He was there.

Philip and June had come forward to stand beside Apple, who, from the edge of his vision, noted with pleasure that the girl was on the tall side. Five feet eight at least, he reckoned. It gave him additional satisfaction that he was able to think of this while knowing that a mission could be in the offing. You'll be a pro yet, he told himself.

"From your conversation," Watkin said dully, addressing the others, "I gather that the gentleman will suffice."

"Yes, sir," the blond man said. He added, "I didn't know you were behind the tree. I didn't realise you were listening."

Then you don't know old Angus, Apple thought with still more pleasure. Our chief loves playing the man of mystery. He'd rather become a uniformed policeman than have any of the underlings know what he's up to.

Watkin said, "One tries to acquire a genuine opinion."

"Quite so, sir."

June spoke. There was less crawl in her voice than in Philip's. "I believe, sir, that the prospect will be perfect. It's simply a matter of technique."

"As you have already pointed out," Watkin said, looking at her as though she were a stepdaughter's poor relation.

"I've seen some of the best." This time she left off the *sir,* to Apple's delight. He mused that she was quite a girl.

Angus Watkin looked back at Philip, saying, "You had a number today, as did the young lady. There was really no urgent need for a formal introduction."

Apple sympathised with the winced, "No, sir, but I—er—"

June said, "Excuse me, sir, but the introduction wasn't all that formal."

Angus Watkin appeared not to have heard. "Good afternoon," he said, easing himself up from his lean on the tree. He turned away. "Come along, Porter."

Apple stepped forward. When he had almost caught up to his chief, who was strolling on, he looked back at June. He sent a smile. She gave a wink.

Two minutes later, walking beside the silent Angus Watkin, Apple again looked back. The blond man had gone. June was still there, watching. She waved. Apple, hoping the act wouldn't be noticed, swung a furtive and awkward arm behind him. He was back facing front as Watkin said, "Stop behaving like a schoolboy, Porter."

"I beg your pardon, sir?"

"Ah, that's better. Guile I approve of. You've never had enough of it. One hopes you are improving."

"Yes, sir," Apple said. He decided against having another look behind.

"And at least," Watkin went on, "you didn't introduce yourself. Though I mustn't be too hard on Seventeen. He didn't give his right name, after all."

"Did the young lady give hers, sir?"

"I haven't the vaguest notion," Angus Watkin said in the tone that Apple recognised as meaning "I know all the circumstances inside out and backwards." "Are we taken by the young lady, perhaps?"

"No, sir. I was curious because of her accent."

"It belongs to one of our former colonies."

"Yes, sir," Apple said, ending the matter diplomatically at that juncture. He knew that Mayflowers came fourth in his superior's list of dislikes, following British Naval Intelligence, the KGB, and cats.

Angus Watkin said, "Accent or not, please be good enough to put the young lady out of your mind. You know the rules."

"I do, sir, yes."

"You will need to observe them even more rigidly than usual from now on, Porter." He paused for effect. "I have a little something for you to do."

Feeling a return of his excitement, Apple said, "Really, sir?" He hoped it sounded blasé, professional, but suspected his voice of playing traitor.

"You will now consider what the forthcoming operation is all about," Angus Watkin said, "and tell me when we reach the road."

After that there was silence as they walked across the grass. Apple didn't waste his time on consideration. If he reached, and gave, a correct conclusion, Watkin would be irked, while he would be putting himself down with one that was wrong. Instead, Apple enjoyed the stroll and his excitement.

In a minute it occurred to him that he had never been as cozy as this before with his chief; never been in such a casual-feeling situation. Their meetings were usually brief and businesslike.

Apple wondered for the first time about Watkin's home life. Did he have a luxury apartment and a glamorous mistress? Did he live in one of the Upstairs buildings, heavily guarded, or out of London in a creepy old mansion? Did he lodge at one of those stuffy clubs in Whitehall? Or did he own a house in some ghastly suburb like Wembley?

They came out of the park onto a main road, Kensington Gore, where traffic on the far side careened by in the rush-hour rage to leave the city. There was a pall of exhaust fumes.

Angus Watkin asked, "Well, Porter?"

"I haven't the vaguest notion," Apple said.

Watkin shot him a curt glance, grunted, quickened his step along the pavement. Apple hoped that his chief didn't know whether to be pleased or not.

They reached a bus stop, where a handful of people waited. As Apple halted there beside Watkin, a double-decker screeched up. The people got aboard. Watkin made no move to follow, and Apple made no mental comment. He was having a fine time.

The bus left. Under the noise of its roar, Angus Watkin said, "The Central Intelligence Agency have one slim finger in this operation, Porter. That much, at least, you have no doubt cleverly figured out."

Wembley, Apple decided. A semi-detached house with a minuscule front garden. The partition wall thin—you could hear every sound from next door, every word of the incessant argu-

ments between the awful, drunken couple who lived there with
their six children.

Apple was smiling inside as he said, "I thought that might be
the case, sir."

He wondered, since Angus Watkin made no answer, if there
was a possibility of them being under the beam of a direction-
microphone. He stayed silent.

Another double-decker came along and stopped. Apple followed his chief onto the platform and upstairs. Only two of the
long seats that stretched from the side passage were occupied: a
woman near the back, a stout man on the front seat but one.
Watkin went to the front. He sat at the seat's far end, by the
window.

In sitting beside him, Apple took note that the stout man
behind, who sat at the passage end, had a scar on one cheek and
looked to be dozing—eyes closed, head nodding like a large trem-
ble. He was sixty-odd and dressed shabbily.

Already Apple was at work playing the observant field operative. He wished he had taken notice of the woman at the rear.
After all, for anything he knew this could be some kind of test.

Quietly, his gaze fixed ahead, Angus Watkin spoke. He said,
"The current password is Haystack."

"Haystack. Right."

"And until I inform you otherwise, your name is Thirty-
four."

"Yes, sir." It was getting better by the second.

"We are using you, Porter, for two reasons."

Apple was musing wryly that, naturally, his chief considered
himself to be above the use of number-names, until Watkin
added, "For your command of Russian and because of your
height."

Apple opened his mouth in surprise. He could hardly believe

that the latter condition was finally doing him a service. It had been the bane of his life.

"Height more than language, in fact," Angus Watkin said. "For perfection in Russian is not particularly vital here. But we do need those long legs—or stems, as the young lady phrased it. So quaint, these Americans."

His excitement mounting, Apple craved a smoke. His need grew deeper as he saw the litter of cigarette butts on the floor. He followed the trail wistfully; then, in looking up from there, saw the stout man's reflection in the window.

To Apple, it appeared as though the man had moved. He had either slumped farther forward in his doze or had moved closer in from the end of the seat. Apple told himself he could be wrong. He turned back at a murmur.

"I beg your pardon, sir?"

"I asked how you scored in memorising."

Apple was tempted to lie with a ten. He felt sure, however, that Angus Watkin would have sent for his dossier before coming to this meeting. He said, "Nine, sir. But that was years ago. I've improved since then."

"Really?" Watkin drawled. "How curious. It usually works the other way around—decline with age. Never mind. Your nine ought to be good enough."

Apple glanced at the side window. The man with the scarred cheek appeared to have slid still farther along the seat and to be drooping lower.

Again Apple tried to tell himself that he could be wrong. It was his excitement, or his eagerness to play spook, or his craving for a cigarette. The try failed. The stout man was definitely edging closer to the pair in front.

"We are going to send you out, Porter," Watkin said softly.

"I see," Apple said, inattentive.

"You will be meeting an informant. He is a Russian national. He speaks no other language but his own, and that with poor grammar."

Nervous, Apple risked disapproval with, "Would you mind if I smoked, sir?"

His superior tutted. "Filthy habit. However, do smoke if you have to." He nodded. "As a matter of act, it's rather a good idea."

"It is?"

"Yes, Porter. The cigarette will be your last."

Less inattentive, Apple asked, "My what, sir?"

"Your last smoke. At least for the time being."

Apple, fumbling to get out packet and lighter: "I don't think I understand, sir." He glanced back, this time not using the window. The scar-cheeked man was now almost directly behind him. His eyes were still closed, his head was still nodding.

Angus Watkin said, "You will smoke no more cigarettes after this one. Your heart and lungs have to be in top condition. Therefore, your weakness for tobacco has to be conquered. Smoking is out. That, Porter, is an order."

Apple flicked on his lighter. He lit up and drew hungrily at the smoke before saying a dull, "Yes, sir." He wondered if the order could be followed. The last time he had tried to give up cigarettes, he had retired defeated after three hours. But the wonder was brief. He was more concerned about the man behind. Should he mention him to his chief? Was the man simply drunk and restless?

"Two days from now," Angus Watkin said, "you will be at Damian House. You will undertake a fortnight of intensive training."

"In which department, sir?" Apple asked, doing so with half his mind given to the drunk or dozing or covertly listening man. He had spoken in a whisper.

"There's no need to hiss at me like that," Watkin said peevishly.

"Excuse me."

"The department is athletics. Which is to say running. You can, it would appear, run. After a fashion. You are going to be taught how to do it properly. All right?"

"Yes, sir."

"In particular, you will be shown how to run the three-thousand-metres race. That's about two miles, or so I'm told. These things are over my head."

Apple was so surprised by that admission, on top of being bewildered by the other information, that he forgot the man with the scar. He blurted, "Why?"

His superior looked at him coolly. "Why what? Why are these things over my head?"

"No. Why am I going to be trained or taught or whatever to run the three thousand metres?" After a blink of time he tacked on, "Sir."

Angus Watkin's eyes grew a shade sleepier, which, as Apple knew, meant he was enjoying himself, now by handing out surprises. He said, "Because, Porter, you will be running that race, in public, in just over two weeks from now. The stadium is at Liverpool. The event is the British Isles finals."

"Oh," Apple said. He took a deep, deep draw on his cigarette.

"Which, of course, makes you none the wiser."

He shook his head, still bewildered. "Perhaps I'm supposed to guess. Or maybe I'm a bit slow today. I don't see the connexion."

"What connexion?"

"What a Russian spiller has to do with a British track-and-field meet in Liverpool. Or anywhere else in this country, for that matter."

"All further information you will be given in due course. By which I mean in safe sequence."

"He must be with the Russian Embassy here."

"He is in Moscow," Angus Watkin said. "But that is not to the point. For the moment, please get it into your head that you are going to win the Liverpool race."

"Win? Against the best in the country?"

"Yes. You will win. That's another order."

"But—"

"You have long legs, Porter, and two weeks. You will use both to ensure success."

"But—"

"Don't burn your fingers."

Apple, though yearning for a last drag, that super-rich intake from the end, exhibited his dubious will by dropping the butt to the floor and topping it firmly with his shoe.

He asked, "What about cover, sir?" It was the only sensible-sounding question he could think of. He felt lost.

"We're working on that," Watkin said. "It might be ready to-night, it might take another week. All you have to worry about is the race, and, needless to say, getting a fortnight's leave of absence from that place you work in—without, let me caution, being too outlandish in your story."

"That's going to be the easiest part," Apple said absently. "I've got several weeks of holiday due to me. I've been letting them build up." He was thinking that this just had to be another of Angus Watkin's quirky deals. The idea of a raw beginner winning against the country's best was absurd.

"Fine," Watkin said. "And that, Porter, is all for the moment." He began to get up. As Apple started to do the same he said, "No, keep your place. Get off at the stop after this one."

"Very good, sir."

"You'll be contacted. Good afternoon."

"Good afternoon, sir," Apple said, and, as Watkin went by and on to the passage, remembered the man with the scar, for he heard his chief ask, "How's the wife, Burton?"

A voice answered, "A lot better, sir, thank you. It wasn't as serious as we thought at first."

"Good. I'm delighted. Follow me off, please, and then go your own way. Good day to you, Burton."

"Good day, sir."

By the next evening, Apple had got part of the operation figured out, as he had the reason for the stout agent's presence on the bus. He had also arranged to take his accumulated vacation time, starting immediately, by telling his superior at the United Kingdom Philological Institute, Professor Warden, that he wanted to go to San Sebastian for a firsthand soaking in Basque. The old man, who was fluent in fourteen languages, had been enthusiastic as well as agreeable.

What Apple had failed to succeed in doing was recover from the trauma of giving up cigarettes. It and the craving thrived.

The first two hours had been easy. It had taken him that long to reach home, 12 Harlequin Mansions, Bloomsbury, for he went on a wide circuitous wander in order to mull the situation over.

Once in his apartment, however, the desire to smoke had erupted in him strongly. His whole being was affected, body and mind and emotions. Smoking was as much a part of him as his personality, or his thoughts, or his fingers. Twice he caught himself in the unconscious act of putting a cigarette to his lips.

Bravely, Apple had ripped the almost-full packet into pieces and flushed it down the lavatory. He did the same with every other packet and stray cigarette he came across during a flurried, frantic, stumbling search around the flat—an exact repeat, but with reverse intentions, of those late-night times when he had opened a packet only to find it empty.

Every flushing had caused him a deep regret. It was like saying good-bye to a friend. At one stage his eyes grew misty. With the last discovery, in one of his emergency hiding places, the finger of a glove (he had happily used gambits learned in Training Six), Apple hesitated over the lavatory bowl. The hand that held the cigarette trembled, while the other, pocketed, was clutched tightly around his lighter.

But Apple did not give in to temptation. He flushed the elongated white pearl away with jutted jaw and glaring eyes, playing the man of iron will. From that he sagged into a mournful droop. A whole battalion of friends had passed away in the space of a few minutes.

Apple's abstinence was due only in part to the order he had been given by Angus Watkin. He wanted to do his best at Damian House. And for that, he knew, his lungs would have to be cleared of fug. He would need to be at his all-round physical finest.

He had spent a curious evening at home, bouncing back and forth between highs and lows. To help beat the craving, he turned his thoughts on other matters. Which meant the coming operation. This teased and excited him so much that he was sent back to an aching yearn for a smoke. He needed two tranquilisers to help him fall asleep.

In regard to the agent called Burton, Apple had reasoned that he had been on the bus for two purposes: first, to ensure privacy and security for the talk between his chief and Appleton Porter; second, to establish Porter in his mind, by both sight and sound. It was on account of the latter that Burton had inched closer, wanting to get every vocal nuance, the timbre, the speech. Obviously, Apple had not seen the last of the stout, scar-cheeked agent. That, in any case, had already been made plain by Watkin having used his name in Apple's hearing—not only once, but twice.

Apple avoided dwelling on the tactical details behind Burton being there on the bus, and refused to think of him continually getting on and off double-deckers and hurrying back between rides, until the expected pair of men finally appeared. Apple didn't want to spoil the dramatic fact of Burton's presence and smooth performance.

As far as the operation was concerned, Apple had figured it out as one more of Angus Watkin's convoluted capers, the old now-you-see-it, now-you-don't. There would be no race at Liverpool, though Apple had to pretend that he believed there would be. But certainly physical fitness must be involved, and possibly even a Russian informant.

Also, that the operation was of consequence showed in the arranging of elaborate preliminaries: the telephone call about the supposed rendezvous on Bayswater Road, Philip and June and their bag-snatching act, Watkin putting in a personal appearance, the stout Burton. A real mission was ahead.

Apple was excited. Apple was wretched.

Today had been the high-low of yesterday evening all over again. Gasping in his need for the usual post-breakfast smoke, Apple had left the apartment and strode all the way to the Philological Institute. After settling vacation matters there, keeping his eyes off the secretaries with their dangling cigarettes, which is not what he generally found of interest about the girls, he set off walking. He decided that he would spend all day away from home, where the bouquet of tobacco was a painful reminder.

But everything was a reminder, Apple had found, as he walked, lunched, visited the National Portrait Gallery, saw a double feature twice, walked, had dinner, and walked. Everyone in London seemed to smoke. Waiters smoked. People made out of oil on canvas smoked. Actors on the screen were incessantly either lighting up or stubbing out. Even women on the streets smoked.

It had been a hard day, with powerful temptations to buy and indulge coming at least every half hour.

Now, Apple was suffering through his latest urge. The East End pub, at nine o'clock, had a good crowd. Apple tried not to look at any of the people around him. All of them were smoking, as was the barmaid, who had dimples.

Apple, swallowing saliva, gave his mind to June. He had thought of her frequently since Kensington Gardens, though not in regards to what she represented in the operation. That she was the CIA's slim finger in the pie was good enough for the moment. That meant he would be seeing her again.

Apple smiled, thinking about the girl herself, her tanned and attractive appearance, her earnest eyes, the way she had responded to Angus Watkin.

Feeling a tingle of anticipation, Apple reached in his pocket for cigarettes. He remembered, groaned under his breath, lifted his glass. But even the usually satisfying sherry on the rocks, his favourite drink, seemed to have a different flavour, as had the food he had eaten today. Not worse; just different.

Apple told himself gamely that his taste buds were coming back to life. Soon, a whole new world of flavours would be opened up to him. Not only that, if he could keep off tobacco permanently, he would add years to his life. Smoking was idiotic.

Apple raised his eyes. He looked with a pity-tinged derision at the people around him. He shook his head at the way they drew deeply on their cigarettes, held them possessively close to their mouths, blew out long streams of smoke.

As Apple continued to watch, his head-shaking stopped. His derision died. The pity turned toward himself. He whimpered.

Apple put down his glass and quickly made his way to the door. Outside, he inhaled the dank, lifeless, and smokeless air before he set off briskly walking.

Dusk was grading into darkness. The street, broad, was drab and semi-commercial, small businesses between tenement blocks. The lighting was as poor as an old prostitute, like some of those who whispered to Apple as he went by the doorways they were using as shells. He was glad his pity had somewhere else to go.

There was a scattering of pedestrians. From some came the glow of lighted cigarettes. One man stopped to flare a match alive and puff at his pipe.

Apple lowered his eyes to the ground. He kept his mind busy by counting how long it had been since he had had a smoke. The sum was twenty-seven hours and—checking his watch—seventeen minutes. His lungs, he mused with grim cheer, were that much better off.

Apple came level with the mouth of an alley. As he did, his downturned vision met the bottom part of a man, who was coming to a stop directly in his path. Apple slowed and looked up. The man was holding a cigarette.

He asked, "Got a light, mate?"

Sighing, Apple halted. While reaching for his lighter he noted with indifference that the man was about his own age, unshaven, wearing gumboots and oil-stained coveralls.

When he heard the rush of movement behind him, Apple brought his hand out of his pocket at the same moment as he flung himself sideways.

Apple took two long, leaping strides into the alley's mouth. Stopping, he swung around. There were two of them now. The second man was the same age as the other, had the same stubble of beard, but wore a cheap-looking green suit. They were both around the six-foot mark and had broad shoulders.

"What's all this?" Apple asked. The words came out firm and stern despite the quickened tempo of his heart.

Side by side, separated by a yard of space, the men began to move slowly forward. Their arms were raised slightly. Each man had a quiet smile, which Apple found more disturbing than grimness would have been.

Nodding, Green-suit said, "Take it nice and easy, mate. That's my advice."

Apple was walking backwards at a steady pace. He said, "You've made a mistake."

Coveralls: "Mistake?"

"I'm not whoever you think I am." He was telling himself that this must be some kind of East End gangland strife.

"What we fink," Coveralls said, "is none of your business."

"Good. So you can both get lost."

His smile spreading, Green-suit said, "I like 'em when they're cheeky."

"Yeah, me too. Adds a bit of spice."

They were still moving forward, at the same speed that Apple was going in reverse. Green-suit had started to wriggle his fingers, as though he had a piano on either side of him. Coveralls had his hands clenched into fists.

He said, "If you just stand still a minute, mate, it'll all be over in no time at all."

Green-suit: "You'll be fine and dandy, and the both of us'll be on our way, getting lost."

Apple asked, "What're you after?"

"Well, as to that," Coveralls said, "it ain't a light."

Which reminded Apple of the darkness. He was going deeper into it, away from the street. But there would be another street at the alley's other end.

With a snapped jerk of his head, Apple looked beyond the stalking pair and shouted, "Hey, you there!"

The men twisted their upper bodies around.

Apple turned the other way. And ran.

He raced along the dim alley. It was nine feet wide and sided with sheer walls. Few lights showed in the buildings' windows, and those were high above ground level.

Behind Apple sounded a clatter of footfalls, from a single pair of feet: the gumboots made no noise other than a curious, rhythmic squeaking, which increased for Apple the strangeness of the situation.

He spared no thoughts for the possible motives or intentions of the two men. His mind at the moment was given fully to one goal: the best way of escaping.

But the way ahead was growing dimmer. There was no sign of a brightness that would mean another street. Apple thought that the alley could be a dead end. Possibly that's why its mouth had been chosen as the place of interception.

He came to a V-junction. Strong light showed to the left. He went that way, running easily. He had lengthened the gap between himself and the men, he could tell: their clatter and squeaking were fainter.

Apple passed through an open gateway—and saw that he had cornered himself. He was in an enclosed yard. The light came from one large, naked bulb above the closed door of a warehouse. There were stacks of cardboard cartons, each pile rising to the height of a house.

Apple stopped and turned. From Training Four he remembered *Do the unexpected.* So, as the men came hurtling through the gateway, he charged straight at them.

He nearly made it. He was passing between the pair when Coveralls took his arm in link fashion and held on tight. The man was heavy as well as on the move. He and Apple, clamped together, swung into a twirl like part of a barn dance.

Swept free by impetus, Apple lurched away. Green-suit was

waiting and ready. He threw a punch. It snapped short several inches from Apple's chin.

Regaining his balance, Apple swung down a karate chop. It made a good connexion with the shoulder muscle. It also sent a charge of pain up Apple's arm. He was badly out of practice. The edge of his hand had gone soft.

Green-suit, even while drooping sideways from the chop's damage, brought around his other arm in a punch to the body. Apple got another jolt of pain, in his ribs.

As he sagged, he heard a rapid squeaking. He straightened fast, along with an uppercut. His fist landed thuddingly on Green-suit's eye. The man swayed back, one leg raising like a lazy kick.

Apple had barely enough time to grab the foot and heave it upwards—sending Green-suit into a backwards fall—before turning to meet the rush of Coveralls.

There was a flurry of useless blows from both sides. Then the man grabbed lapels and tried that favourite East End trick of tupping. He wasn't tall enough—his head butted against Apple's chest. For the second time in a little over twenty-four hours, Apple was glad of his height.

With a quick, opening X of forearms, he broke the hold on his lapels. He brought the spread hands back together, thumbs out and rigid. His ploy failed, though it had always worked in the gym, on opponents with eye-guards. Coveralls simply bent at the knees. Apple's hands met each other painfully.

They hurt again as, by accident, they blocked a punch thrown by the man. Another punch was already on its way. Apple dodged. He took a double hold on the arm, twisted it up while ducking beneath, and heaved.

This time the ploy worked. The man's feet left the ground. He rose in the air, not quite perpendicular, but good enough to give Apple a thrill of success. It helped balance his fear.

Coveralls landed and rolled. At the same moment, a blow crashed onto the back of Apple's neck. He staggered forward, toward Coveralls, who was on his hands and knees, and ended his stagger by throwing a kick at the bent head. He missed.

Turning, he went toward the other man. He was telling himself that they were unskilled in the finer points of dirty fighting and that he ought to have had them both out of action by this time. He also thought how lucky he was that they were unarmed. He might have had knives or razors to deal with.

Green-suit came in with both arms pumping like pistons. Apple tapped him off with straight lefts, then brought over and down a powerful right-hander. It scored on the man's brow, but the blow had little effect. The arms were still pumping.

From behind came again the squeak of gumboots. Apple shunted aside. As he did, both men reached him with shoving hands. He went reeling away in semi-reverse.

Apple held his breath while he fought to stay upright. His fear was strong. He knew that if he fell, he was finished. Flailing his arms, he managed to keep his balance as well as maintain his distance from the fast-following pair of men.

Apple neared a tower of cartons. The wall would hold him up, he knew with relief. He prepared himself for the shock of arrival. But when he hit the wall, it was with a softened impact. The cartons were empty.

The tower collapsed. Boxes came tumbling down. They fell around Apple and the men, and went on falling. One landed neatly over the head of Green-suit. He hit himself on the cheek while punching it off. Neither he nor the other man were now smiling. Apple hadn't noticed that before. They looked determined, ruthless.

They also looked silly, and Apple supposed he did himself. The three of them were thigh-deep in cubes of cardboard two feet square. Boxes were still falling.

Coveralls tried to wade forward, his fists raised. He tripped and went down. With a grind of cardboard, he disappeared into the mass of boxes.

Hands above to ward off the falling cartons, which had hard corners, Apple raised one long leg. He headed off to the side as he took huge, high strides. Green-suit was beginning to follow until his partner, who had just come back into view, grabbed him for balance. Snarling, they both fell.

Apple went on calmly with his long and high strides. When his shoe met a box, he scuffled about until he found his way past it to the ground. The level started to sink. After three more strides he was able to kick his way through. He got clear altogether with a final leap.

Apple looked back. Green-suit and Coveralls were wobbling about in their efforts to wade after him in pursuit. He blew them a kiss, turned and ran for the gate.

Half an hour later, Apple had left the East End behind and was nearing Bloomsbury. He had alternated running with brisk walking. His nerves were still settling from the encounter, but he had been able to do some clear cogitating. He had reached certain conclusions with regard to the two unshaven men.

One, they were muggers.

Two, they were involved in some kind of gang warfare and had taken him for somebody else.

Three, mistaken identity again, they were out to fulfil a contract for GBH—Grievous Bodily Harm—or even murder.

Four, they were insane.

Five, they were Hammers.

There were no other possibilities—at least, none that Apple could think of. With the exception of Four, they were all equally probable. Only Five presented a problem. Apple worked on it as he strode between bursts of running.

At last he turned into his own street. He crossed toward the sedate Edwardian building called Harlequin Mansions. On the pavement, nearing, he noted that a man was leaning on the side of a car that was parked close to the entrance. Apple tensed.

The man saw him. He moved away from the car and stood in the centre of the pavement. Folding his arms, he stood in a casual droop. He looked to be bored with being impatient.

When Apple had drawn almost level, the man said, "I've been waiting hours." He was about thirty, well dressed, with an average build and a forgettable face.

Apple stopped. "Is that right?"

"We've been trying to ring you all day."

"We have, have we?"

"Hello, Thirty-four," the man said. "Haystack."

"It might have been a good idea if you'd started with that in the first place."

The man shrugged. He cocked his head, peering. "You look a bit ruffled and rent, old man. Look as though you've been pulled through a hedge backwards."

Apple smoothed down his hair and touched his tie. The knot was off-centre. Straightening it, he said, after a brief hesitation, "I've been running."

The man blinked. "Running?"

Which, Apple thought, meant that he didn't know anything. He was only a courier. "I like to run."

"You should wear a track suit."

"It's none of your business what I wear," Apple snapped. He then felt ashamed of himself. He was pulling rank. It occurred to him with disgust that, if he ever got into a position of power, he would be every bit as awful as Angus Watkin.

Apple smiled weakly as he realised that his curt response must have been a withdrawal symptom, the classical bad-temperedness.

"Just trying to be friendly," the man said, shrugging again. He betrayed no emotion. "I have a message for you."

"All right."

"A car will pick you up here on the street at ten o'clock tomorrow morning."

"Fine. Any signals?"

"No signals needed," the man said, dropping his arms from their fold. He moved forward and went on by. "Good night, Russet."

Apple clenched his fists at the use of the hated nickname. But it serves me right, he thought. Tit for tat. Who am I to go snapping at people? And no, I could never be like Watkin in a million years. I hope.

Ignoring the entrance to his block of flats, Apple began to stroll. He also ignored the renewed craving for a cigarette. He was thinking about that hesitation a moment ago. It seemed to have said that he had resolved his problem.

Although Green-suit and Coveralls had fought like mere tough guys, that didn't cancel out the possibility of them being Hammers. They could have been deliberately putting on an act, leaving out everything they knew about unarmed combat, certainly until it was plain that the victim wouldn't get away to tell the tale.

And, if KGB they were, or even mere hirelings of same, not true Hammers, it could only mean that Appleton Porter had been rumbled—in his connexion with the coming operation. Which in turn meant that if he told Watkin about the unshaven pair, he would be pulled out so fast he wouldn't have time to say good-bye.

Apple nodded. He didn't care about Angus Watkin and his convoluted games. He did care about being out in the field, an agent on a mission. That was all that mattered. Therefore, no one would be told about Coveralls and Green-suit.

Satisfied, Apple turned to head back for home. In a doorway, a couple were lighting cigarettes. Apple started to run.

CHAPTER 2

It was another beautiful day. The car, an inconspicuous grey Rover several years old, went at a leisurely pace along the country road. On either hand were meadows where sheep grazed and cows displayed their eternal complacency. The car's driver was Burton.

He had arrived at Harlequin Mansions two minutes after Apple, carrying an overnight bag, had emerged from the building. Burton had leaned across and unlatched the rear door, saying, "Good morning. Hop inside. We'll talk when we get out of the city traffic. Driving in London isn't good for my stomach."

Burton looked younger today, as if on the double-decker bus he had deliberately played the older man. His round face had a cheery aspect. He was wearing a natty blue suit and a bowtie with polka dots. He could have passed for a real estate agent taking a customer to see a property.

Despite his hinted injunction against conversation, there had been sporadic talk on the long drive through one suburb after another. At one stage, stopping at lights, Burton had said, "I'm Twenty-nine in this caper, by the way. But call me Bill, eh?"

"I'm Apple." The number meant that Burton had been brought into the operation five people before him. He wondered where CIA June stood on the list.

During another lull, Apple had asked, "How did you get that scar on your cheek, Bill?"

The driver showed a grin in profile. "Fell on a broken bottle when I was knee-high to a flea. But it's done me a lot of good. It helps no end when I turn on the sinister routine."

Waiting out a minor traffic jam, Burton had looked behind via the rearview mirror. "Does that ease the pain?"

"A bit," Apple said, speaking around the matchstick that he was giving a thorough chew. His craving for a smoke was as strong as ever. He didn't know how he had survived his post-breakfast need.

"I gave up cigs years ago, with the help of hypnosis. If I'd been a smoker, I wouldn't be here in this car with you today."

"No, I don't suppose dear Watkin goes in for anything as harsh as torture."

"Don't be too sure about that. With old Angus you never know."

Apple had taken a liking to Bill Burton.

Steering the car around a gentle curve, the stout man now said, "Okay, down to cases. First your cover. Ready to absorb, Thirty-four?"

"Yes, sir."

"Your name is Appleton Porter, a bachelor, a linguist, you live in Bloomsbury, and you're a civil servant."

Apple smiled. "Are you putting me on?"

Bill Burton shook his head. "Your cover is you. The one you already have. That was settled days ago."

"Watkin said it wasn't ready yet."

"I heard. I wasn't surprised. He likes everything in sequence regarding the need to know. I must admit he's right. That's one of the reasons why he's up there and we're down here."

Apple was disappointed about the lack of new cover. This, he felt, could mean an insignificant operation. But he reminded himself of all the preliminary elaborations.

He said, "I don't get it."

Burton glanced in the mirror. "That track meet in Liverpool. The media will be there—press, radio, television. Forget the middle one. The others will show stills and films. See what I mean?"

"I'm bound to be seen by someone who knows me," Apple said, though he still didn't believe in the race. "And wearing a disguise would be difficult."

"Our makeup department is pretty slick, but when someone's charging around and sweating, there's a big risk of the phoney face falling apart. Nothing short of plastic surgery would be A-1 secure."

"I can do without that, thank you."

"I'm with you there. Spare me doctors."

Apple put his frayed and soggy matchstick in the ashtray. Slowly, relishing the ritual, he brought from his pocket a box of matches, which he poked open with a forefinger, needing several taps to complete the job.

Selecting a matchstick with care, as if they were not all alike, he held it between his first two fingers while closing the box and putting it away, then languidly tapped its sulphur head on his thumbnail.

After lifting the other end to his lips, he began, "That race."

Bill Burton nodded. "It's arranged for you to run. Your name was entered yesterday morning."

Although he still didn't believe it, Apple's thoughts went in a different direction. He had been listed as an entrant in the morning, and accosted by Green-suit and Coveralls that same night. Which gave strength to the theory of KGB involvement. But he was still going to keep mum.

"There's more to your cover than simply you, of course," Bill Burton said. "There's leisure activity. You can't spring into the world of sport out of nowhere, without some kind of provable athletic background."

Apple drew the matchstick in to his teeth and began to chew. "No, that wouldn't work."

"You're a member of the Civil Service Harriers, and you'll be given a bent-eared card to prove it. The club does exist. But you've been going there early mornings over the past few months, training in semi-secret. You didn't think you were any good. Only five of the senior officials know about your membership. They've been squared, needless to say."

Apple had lost his disappointment. He chewed well around. "Naturally."

"You thought you were maybe marathon material," Burton went on. "That's what you were training for, the endurance stuff. Then a runner happened to be there one morning, guesting from another club. He's a three-thousand-metres man. He asked you to do the seven and a half laps with him—a lap is four hundred metres, in case you're not aware of that."

"I'm not. I know damn all about this track stuff, apart from the famous names."

"You'll get a cram course, don't worry."

"But then, if I'm a shy beginner who underrates himself, it isn't likely I'd be hot on details."

"That's a good point," Burton said. "Anyway, you kept pace with this runner, who used to be a bit of a star, and on the last circuit he found to his surprise that he couldn't leave you behind. That annoyed him so much that he really pulled out all the stops. He did beat you, but only just. Everything happened from there. It was May seventh, about a month ago, on a Tuesday morning."

"Check," Apple said. "What was the weather like?"

"Gloomy and damp. The runner's name is John Wardle. You know him as Philip, incidentally. There are other names, plus descriptions, that you're going to have to know: those officials at the club. Pin back your ears, Apple."

"Pinned and waiting."

For ten minutes, speaking at a steady pace, Bill Burton gave out information. It included addresses, personal habits, mannerisms, past achievements in amateur sports, political leanings, positions present or past in the civil service.

The reason Apple concentrated hard, taking it all in, was because he knew the data would be needed—though probably not by anyone who suspected the cover story. The information could even be totally invented. But soon someone would ask questions about the Harriers, and he would have to give the correct answers. This was a memory test.

Finishing, Bill Burton said, "Absorbed, Thirty-four?"

"To the last facial tic, Twenty-nine. They sound odd enough to be real."

Burton shot him a glance via the mirror. He said, "We'll be there in a minute."

Damian House was a massive piece of masonry. Of the late Georgian period, it consisted of a main body and two wings. Its entrance, up broad steps, lay under a curving, pillared portico. The building was impressive and attractive, but it seemed designed to please the eye, not to provide a home.

The park-like grounds covered twenty acres. Some sections were used to grow vegetables, others were for fowl. In one place near the rim there was a circular track, cindered, with an inner wooden rail to make it look as if it were meant for horses.

39

Only a low and bedraggled hedge surrounded the property. Anything more formidable—high walls, fences, dogs—would have been a sign of the truth. But the hedge did have concealed warning-signal wires.

Close to the house there were sweeping lawns, the obligatory maze, statuary, greenhouses, a large swimming pool with diving boards on three levels, tennis courts, and a cricket pitch. It all looked totally normal.

To the local farmers and the people of Little Wentworth, a village three miles away, the estate was without interest. They believed its cover, that it was a holiday centre for Armed Forces personnel and their families. Nothing ever happened there.

For fifty years, Damian House had been operated by the Intelligence services, for hospitalisation, convalescence, and some of the less dangerous training courses. In one wing, unhidden from the innocent visitor, there was a fully equipped gymnasium. In a basement, well hidden from sight and ear, was a shooting range. Also hidden were cells, interrogation rooms, radio transmitters, and a stock of lifelike dummies which had been strangled and crippled and stabbed ten thousand times.

The Rover went along the gravel driveway and came to a stop in front of the steps. Apple got out, followed by Bill Burton. As they went up under the portico, Apple saw that the stout man was also carrying a bag.

He asked, "You're staying here as well?"

"There's one thing I forgot to mention," Burton said. "I'm your back-up man on this caper."

"Well," Apple said, "it's nice to know these minor details." He mused with pleasure that the operation was getting bigger all the time. On small jobs, no one got a back-up.

They passed through into the expansive hall. Spaced about were leather couches and armchairs, where lounged twenty-odd people of all ages from twenty up, a quarter of them women.

They looked at the newcomers with the studied disinterest that was taught in Training Four.

The small, older man behind the reception desk didn't try to disguise his curiosity. All staff at Damian House loved playing spy. He nodded with narrowed eyes and satisfaction when Bill Burton said, "We'd like rooms thirty-four and twenty-nine, please, if they happen to be available."

After repeating the numbers with emphasis, the clerk said, "Sorry, sir, they're taken. But I can give you others just as nice." He slid forward a closed register, on which lay two keys. "You won't be disappointed."

Apple and Burton unisoned, "Thank you," took a key apiece, and headed for the broad staircase, down which, years before, Apple had fallen in a state of drunken helplessness during his trial of tolerance for alcohol.

He mentioned that event as they climbed. Bill Burton said smugly, "I'm a ten myself."

"Congratulations. I'll buy you a drink later."

"No you won't. We're both off the grog. I go this way. See you at lunch, though only at a distance."

Bigger and bigger, Apple mused happily, continuing alone along the passage. But if Bill Burton was typical of the average operative, he wouldn't obey the order against drinking. He would bribe the bartender to sneak him drinks, as well as smuggling a bottle up to his room.

Apple let himself into a bedroom that was small and simply furnished. On the table beside the prim single bed were a water carafe and glass, a pile of mystery novels, and an alarm clock. There was no ashtray. Sighing, Apple sat down to go through the vaguely comforting ritual of getting out a matchstick to chew.

An hour later, downstairs, Apple strolled into the dining room, where the service was cafeteria style. About to get himself a tray, he stopped when a white-coated steward asked, "It's room thirty-four, sir, isn't it?"

It wasn't, but his designation was. Apple said, "That's right."

"If you'd care to find yourself a place, sir, I'll see that you're served."

Having a hard job not to raise his eyebrows in surprise, Apple moved away from the counter and looked around. As he was a little late, all the side tables were taken. No agent, tyro or pro, ever lost the opportunity to get the maximum both in safety for his back and scan for his vision, as Apple knew, just as he knew that with the old-timers it was an unconscious act, a habit.

He got out his box of matches while choosing a table in the middle. Bill Burton, he saw, was sitting near the row of diamond-leaded windows, beside a man his own age who had a bottle of wine. Burton had a non-transparent cup.

Apple sat. The steward was there immediately with a jug of milk, brown bread, a glass of carrot juice, and a salad. From the attention he could feel focussed on him, Apple guessed that the fact of these items not being on the set menu was causing as much interest as the personal service. He would have felt uncomfortable except for being achingly hungry.

The second course was a huge steak, totally lean, kept company by one bake-jacket potato and one boiled onion. The attention from around the room seemed to take on an essence of reproach. The food at Damian House, it was claimed, had been the reason for more than one aspiring spy deliberately failing the course.

As his plate was being replaced by a bowl of fresh diced fruit with ice cream, Apple saw with admiration that the man beside Bill Burton was pouring wine into the cup while keeping the bottle completely hidden behind his forearm.

What Apple next saw, beyond the men, was CIA June. She was walking past the windows.

Despite being tense, Apple put on an easy air as he got up. He moved around the steward and went toward the doorway. Reaching there, he glanced back. June, heading in the opposite direction, was just going from sight by the last window.

In the hall, which was deserted save for the desk clerk, Apple dropped his act. He strode briskly to an arch and along a corridor. He went into the first room he came to. It was for storage. He went right on to the end, passing other rooms, until he came to a turning, which led him to an exterior door.

Outside quickly, Apple looked around. There was no one to be seen, except a man in the distance who was rolling the cricket pitch. Apple went on to the corner of the building, still saw no one, came back and tried the one other exterior door on this facade. It was locked.

A mirage, Apple told himself as he returned indoors. A delusion. Hallucination due to being starved of nicotine.

Even so, he stopped by the desk before going back to his dessert. He asked, "Is there an American girl staying here?"

With a face and vocal tone of total incredulity, the desk clerk said, "*American?*"

The man who was waiting outside the dining room showed his rank immediately by a casual, "Hello, Porter. Hope you enjoyed your lunch. I'm Giles Parker."

"How do you do, sir."

They shook hands. Expressionless, Parker said, "You're not going to like me very much, but that can't be helped. I'll be training you. I'm going to turn you into a runner."

"Yes, sir," Apple said. "Thank you."

Giles Parker was tall and with an upright stance. Aged about forty, he had a deep suntan over his baldness and a thin, hawk-like face. His eyes were steady, penetrating. The two middle fingers of his left hand were missing. He wore flannels and a tweed jacket that was fortified with leather on the cuffs, at the elbows, and around the lapels.

"These are for you," he said, producing a small bottle. It held blue pills. "Take one every morning before you get out of bed, when the alarm clock rings at six minus ten."

"Yes, sir," Apple said. He put the bottle in his pocket. "If I'm allowed to ask, what are they for?"

"You are, and the pills will change slightly the rhythm of your heart when you exert yourself. Over a period of time, they would be dangerous. But you won't be taking them for long."

"I see. It's a case of every little bit helps."

"Precisely," Giles Parker said. "Now I want you to go to your room and lie down. Nap if you can. Meet me later this afternoon, at the track, at five o'clock plus nothing."

"Yes, sir," Apple said smartly. He knew a no-nonsense man when he saw one, and Parker scored a ten in that league. It was something that Apple could respect. He thought it unlikely that he would come to dislike the cool, hard-looking trainer.

Four hours later, Apple wasn't so sure about that. Giles Parker had been ordering him around like a convict in a quarry, though remaining stonily calm as opposed to Apple's panting agitation from his labours and smothered annoyance.

They were alone at the oval track, which was out of sight of Damian House. Visible in the distance in that direction was Bill Burton, sitting against a tree. The other way, toward the boundary hedge, a man in overalls was torpidly raking leaves.

"The knees, Porter," Parker said. "Keep them down. You're not a little girl skipping rope. I want to see only the slightest of bending. The legs must be *stretched*. You're not trying for the hundred metres, you know. *Stretch*."

"Yes, sir."

"And don't let me see you make your hands into fists again. That creates an air-block. It feels as if it's helping, I know, but it isn't. Hands flat, Porter. Thumbs down. You've got to slice your way through that barrier of air."

"Yes, sir," Apple said. It was no help to his feelings that, whereas the trainer's grey track suit was a snug fit, his own, of the same colour, tugged high on his wrists and failed to reach his ankles. He knew he looked ludicrous. A cigarette would have helped.

Giles Parker said, "Right. Now off you go on the circuit. Do the seven and a half laps. Keep your pace to the one I set for you."

Apple ran. His trainer, having moved to the middle of the oval, shouted, "Watch those bloody knees!" or, "Hands flat, Porter!" or, "Is that the smoothest you can do?"

It was the same the next day, and the next, and the next. Although Apple believed he understood the psychology—hate the man and so do all you can to prove him wrong in his opinion of your ability—that didn't stop him from taking a healthy dislike to Giles Parker, who seemed totally lacking in human warmth.

The routine never varied. Apple was awakened by the alarm clock ten minutes before six. He swallowed a blue pill, showered, put on the undersized suit and went to the track. After breakfast, at eight, a bored man in an office droned out the history of foot races, starting with Greece. Next came a rest, lunch, a siesta, the main session at the track. When dinner had settled, there was an hour of easy jogging. Bedtime was ten o'clock.

Apple talked to hardly anyone in the house. Bill Burton kept his distance while always being somewhere in the vicinity, indoors or out. Near the track, the leaf-raking man seemed to be making little progress in his work; he covered only a few yards a day. Apple thought he knew the reason why. He was proved right on the fifth afternoon.

Giles Parker had been giving another lecture. It had started after Apple had done his three thousand metres, during which,

on the last lap, he had obeyed the shout of, "Now give it everything!" It had been the first time Parker had asked him to run
full out.

"I've seen schoolboys with better action," the trainer said,
standing with hands on hips, looking down. Apple was flat on
his back, panting. "I was warned about the head-wagging, but I
didn't think it could be that bad."

"Sorry," Apple gasped.

"It's the same as the clenched fists, Porter, only worse. It's
waving a big fat fan at the air. You have to get it out of your
mind that it helps. It does not. What—"

Giles Parker broke off at the sound of a whistle. He looked
around, said, "Stay put," and moved away at an unhurried jog.
Apple raised his head to watch.

Parker passed near the man in overalls, who was intent on his
job of raking. They didn't look at one another. Parker went on
at the same easy gait and in a minute was lost from view behind
bushes.

Apple looked in the other direction. Bill Burton, who had
been in his habitual sitting lean against a tree, was coming forward at a lazy amble. He appeared to be admiring the clouds.

Giles Parker returned within five minutes. He gave a negative
wave to Burton before sinking to a squat. "It's nothing," he said.
"A farm labourer. I know him."

Apple sat up. "It could've been a snooper?"

"You never can tell."

"One of our friendly allies, I suppose."

Parker said, "Or a Hammer."

Apple thought he was joking. "The Reds don't know about
this place, surely."

For the first time in Apple's presence, Giles Parker smiled. He
said, "The boys in Moscow have known about Damian House
for thirty years. They even once wormed an agent in here as a

steward. We have most of their places spotted as well. It's all part of the game."

"A dangerous one, at this particular moment."

"Not really. If they know that we know that they know what the house is used for, then they'll believe we'll keep its activities to the innocent minimum. They won't give it a second thought. They're busy at the moment concentrating on a place of ours near Bristol, where *nothing* ever happens—except the elaborate security arrangements, which everyone there takes seriously because they think it's for real. Forget I said that."

"But the Reds. You don't know if they know that you know that they know?" Apple wasn't sure if he had that right.

Parker shook his head. "We managed to give that agent the sack on genuine-seeming reasons. It was a neat bit of work."

"Sounds like the Angus Watkin type of thing."

The trainer rose with no change in his expression and put his hands on his hips. "Now, as I was saying about the big fat fan . . ."

There was another lecture the following afternoon, another the day after that. Apple got used to the quiet abuse, the way he had grown accustomed to the routine of his days and the personal attention in the dining room. His dislike of Parker thrived on a much lower level than his craving for cigarettes. He chewed matches, grass, fingernails, and, one evening in his bedroom, when his matchbox was empty, the corner of a paperback novel.

Apple had an hour to spare before he went to the track for his afternoon session. He dawdled downstairs to the hall, but once there quickened his pace to leave, going along an off-passage. It wasn't because he felt embarrassed by looking clownish in his undersized track suit; that problem he had solved by keeping the sleeves shoved up above his elbows and by wearing knee socks over the legs. He left the hall for the same reason that he spent little time there socialising. Every other resident was a smoker. Anywhere Apple looked, he saw a cigarette.

He headed for the one sure place, indoors, where no one would be smoking—the gymnasium. One flight of steps took Apple down to a green door. Beside it was a second door of unpainted metal. Once, years before, Apple had heard through the metal, faintly, the sound of sobbing. He hadn't thought further about it then, he gave it no mind now beyond the recollection. Apple didn't want to believe in the seamier side of the espionage trade.

The gym was large. It had a wealth of equipment, including a boxing ring, a springboard, and an ancient, wheel-less Rolls-Royce standing beside a movable belt whose speed could be regulated. During his first time at Damian House, Apple had spent an hour a day learning how to hurl himself from the car onto the simulated road.

In the room's centre lay a large, thick mat. Sitting or standing around it were a dozen or so people, two of them female. They were the same mixed bag as all the residents: novice trainees with keen expressions, convalescents with crutches or slings or gauntness, old campaigners looking sour because they were having to do refresher courses. Most were in shorts and singlets.

On the mat, pushing a burly trainee around as easily as though he were ten years old and getting over measles, was a man in heavy padding. Equally thick were his gloves and the head-guard that resembled a ski hood. He stood with feet spread and arms raised.

Repeatedly, face taut with determination, the novice rushed in to attack, hands chopping or legs kicking. The padded man seemed to make only the slightest of moves, yet his opponent was deflected every time, sent staggering away without having landed a blow.

Apple smiled with amused tolerance. He ignored the fact that in unarmed combat he himself was only a six. Scraping a fingernail on his teeth, he stood on, watching the trainee give up finally and the man in padding beckon another opponent onto the mat.

This one was older and wiser. He didn't rush in. Approaching at a stalking walk, he burst into activity only when he was right in the receiver's territory. Two-thirds of his blows and chops scored. He did beautifully with the double-thumb gouge to the eyes—although, as Apple knew, there was ample protection inside the hood.

With silence both from the combatants and the audience, the fight lasted five minutes. It ended when the man in padding signalled enough. He then, as his opponent strolled off, turned around to face Apple, and beckoned.

After a pause, Apple patted himself on the chest in a question. The man nodded. He said through the hood's mouth-slit, "Yes, you, if you don't mind."

The voice was a shock. It did not belong to a man. It was a female voice with an accent that had been acquired through many expensive terms at an exclusive school. Its affectation was accompanied by the usual nerve-grating high pitch. It was the super-British speech that comics loved to ape and provincials failed to understand.

Apple cleared his throat nervously. He had been enjoying the mystique he had unintentionally created for himself in Damian House, born of his exclusiveness and the specially prepared meals that were served to him personally. This could be reversed if he made a poor showing here. Particularly against a woman.

Apple went forward. He stepped onto the mat. Copying the last opponent, he approached the fighting territory with slow caution. At the penultimate moment he swung his right arm

49

aside, but, instead of using it, threw a straight kick with his left leg.

The toe of his sneaker landed in the ribs. The woman grunted as she was jolted off-balance. Joyful, Apple swept in with the prepared right. His chop connected with the neck of the hood. Again the woman grunted. She went into a sideways stumble.

Apple flung out another kick. His foot missed and his leg went flying high—and the woman disappeared from view. Next thing Apple knew, he was floating in air.

That lasted for no more than two seconds. Then he was landing on the mat, on his back, with a crash that boomed around the room and jarred every bone in his body. He couldn't stop himself yelping.

At his side knelt the woman. Leaning over him, she pulled off the hood and asked anxiously, "You all right?"

"Christ," Apple said. "It's you."

"I guess it is," June said in a low, non-carrying tone. Her accent was back to being standard American. "But are you okay?"

"I know how to land," Apple exaggerated. "I'm fine."

"You're sure? I mean really sure?"

He grinned, taking in the tan, dimples, bubbly hair, and dark eyes. "I never felt better in my life."

"If you're trying to flatter me," June said, "try away. With me it works."

Apple put his hands behind his head as if he didn't hurt in the slightest. He felt like yelping again. He said, "I like dimples."

"Please keep your voice down. I only slipped out of cover because you've already met me."

"I'm probably unconscious and dreaming."

"Get up, you dope. We can talk if we pretend to be doing the mutual instruction bit. Okay?"

While they were both rising, Apple said quietly, "You do the up-nose British accent fabulously. And I'm not flattering you."

"Thanks," June muttered. "I'm a dialectician—in the second sense of the word. Though mimic would be a better term. I can do you any North American accent from Toronto to Phoenix, from the Florida Keys to Seattle. I can even do several dialects from inside West by God Virginia."

"You're a very talented girl."

"Thanks again," June said. "For the girl. At twenty-six I feel I'm not only over the hill but away and climbing the next."

"This is a hard business."

Smiling her dimples deeper, she asked, "Then why don't we all get out of it?" She dropped the smile, shook her head. "Never mind. Not changing the subject, but changing the subject, I hear you're a language freak."

Well, Apple thought, that's better than being a freak of height. He said, "I do know two or three."

"I'm lousy with my foreign languages—Russian and German —except with the accents."

They stood facing one another. Apple, making a slicing gesture with his hand, asked in a low tone, "Is June your real name?"

"Yes, but for the time being, here and elsewhere, I'm Marcia Greystone-Cairn." She lifted the hood and pulled it over her head. "I've heard you referred to as Russet. I'll call you Russ, if you don't mind."

He did. Greatly. He said, "Please do. I'd be delighted."

"We're making progress," June said through the slit of mouth.

Apple nodded happily. "You're staying here, of course. I saw you the other day."

"No, I'm at the pub in Little Wentworth. My Control's

there, too, though he's playing Yank tourist. They let me come here to work out."

"Why don't they let you stay?"

June shrugged her padded shoulders. "The Agency and the Brits are cozy at the moment, sure, but not *that* cozy. I strayed the other day—maybe that's when you saw me—and I was given a rocket by some snotty guy."

"I know how it is. Last year they were bitter enemies, your lot and mine. In three months from now they might not be on speaking terms."

"They're like a bunch of kids."

"Will you be here tomorrow?"

June made a swaying motion with her upper body, as if describing a piece of action. "I'll tell you, Russ, I have no idea. Everything I do is at short notice."

"We're pretty much in the same boat."

From the audience a man called out, "How about giving me a turn, Miss Greystone-Cairn?"

"We have to break this up," June said.

Backing off, Apple murmured, "Will I be seeing you again?"

"You will, Russ. You surely will."

The following session at the cinder track was a good deal less than successful. Apple's mind gave more time to June than to training, and his body still hurt from the fall. Giles Parker was curt and disdainful.

Next morning, when Apple got to the track, he found another man waiting with the trainer, who said, "This is Nineteen. I understand you've already met."

Apple shook hands with the blond, crew-cut man he knew as Philip. He wore a track suit. It looked to have been lovingly made to order on Savile Row.

Parker asked, "Are we a bit more in the mood today, Porter?"

"Yes, sir."

"Good, because you're going to do the three thousand, and you're really going to try. You'll be paced by Nineteen, during the last half. He has a clock in his head. Stay with him. All right?"

"Yes, sir."

"Shall we get on with it, Nineteen?"

The blond man said, "Right you are, sir." He nodded friendlily to Apple, turned and walked off along the track. On the back of his suit, in different colours, were five linked rings.

"Yes," Parker said. "He won a silver at the last Olympics."

Apple said, "Oh."

"He's a miler. Past his peak now, but still a very handy runner. And he still has that clock in his head."

Midway around the track, Philip stopped and sat down. Giles Parker said, "Get on your mark, Porter." He strode away toward the centre of the oval, pulling his sleeve back from his stopwatch as he went.

Apple moved to the scraped line that crossed the cinders. He crouched, watching the trainer. Parker stopped and turned, raised his right arm, looked at his watch. Apple tensed. He moved forward as the arm came down.

Apple ran at a steady, long-loping speed, the one he had been schooled to take. It used up little energy. He felt good, relaxed, despite the competition threat from an Olympic star. He was still sure, in any case, that there was something else behind all this.

Apple passed where Philip was sitting—and envied him the blade of grass in his mouth. It was still there on the next lap, but gone when Apple went by again, still running at his ease.

Parker called, "Step it up slightly, Porter."

Apple increased his speed, though gradually, working up to it as per previous instructions. He saw that Philip had got to his feet and was walking along the track. The walk changed slowly to a jog. The jog soon became a run. The run grew faster as Apple closed the gap.

In a minute, he had drawn level. They moved side by side. The only sound was the snappy crunch of cinders. Apple had his hands correctly flat and was keeping his legs as unbent as possible.

Philip increased his speed. Apple kept abreast. He was no longer running easily. He could feel the exertion in his thighs and lungs. He hoped he wouldn't get a stitch. Whatever the caper might be that lay behind all this, he had to shine.

For the following two laps there seemed to be no change in the star miler's pace. Though suffering, Apple managed to stay at his side. He began to feel a tentative elation.

Giles Parker shouted, "Home stretch!"

Instantly, as if blown by a wind, Philip shot ahead. Apple's jaw dropped. He slammed it up again as he poured on the pressure. He gave everything to the run. Yet Philip not only stayed in front but slowly widened the gap.

Despairing, feeling that his body was about to fall apart, Apple tore in pursuit. His sole consolation was that the gap appeared to be remaining constant.

Philip was twenty yards ahead when he flashed over the finish line. Getting there for Apple was like being kicked all over. He crossed, slowed, weaved to the grass and slumped down into a foetal kneel. He fought for air.

I'm out of the operation, he thought.

Dimly he was aware that Giles Parker had come over and was talking to Philip. The miler gasped, "Yes. He's okay. He'll do."

"The time was nothing special. Were you really trying?"

"Yes, sir. He's fairly good."

"Fine. That's all we need to know."

"And remember," Philip said, "he was running on the outside."

"Yes, the idiot," Giles Parker said. "Porter?"

Apple straightened, sat back on his heels. He was breathing a mite easier. "Sir?"

"I did tell you about that. Running on the outside adds an immense amount of yardage to the distance you're covering. Cuddle the inner line of the track."

"Sorry, sir, I forgot." He frowned as if in regret, even though he felt like grinning. He was in.

"Keep ahead of your man, or, far better, stay behind. Stay right behind. Chase him. Worry him. Frighten him. Breathe down his neck. Stay as close as you can."

"But what if I step on his heels?"

Giles Parker smiled. "That would be too bad for the poor soul, wouldn't it?"

"Ah," Apple said. "Yes." He answered the smile but didn't feel that way.

"Right. Now we're going to teach you the final fling, that head-first swoop near the tape. It's a skill that's won more races than sheer speed. On your feet, Porter."

Later that evening, after dinner, Apple left the house to jog. He went his usual way, past the tennis courts. Glances back showed him that Bill Burton was ambling along behind. Apple was thinking about the village of Little Wentworth.

Cutting out his siesta, he had spent the afternoon sitting in the gymnasium. June had not put in an appearance. But the village was only three miles away. It would be an easy run there and back, with a good two hours of daylight left. No one would be the wiser. He often left Burton out of sight, sometimes for as much as thirty minutes. This would take longer than that, but he could shrug it off. Burton might not even know of June's existence, thanks to Angus Watkin's love of secrecy.

Apple thought about it.

He rounded a cluster of service sheds. Ahead stood a clump of trees. It would give excellent cover for the open stretch of lawn that came next, before the far patch of woodland.

Apple stopped thinking about it.

From around the last shed had strolled one of the groundsmen. He was using both hands to carry a coiled hose. In his lips was a cigarette. He looked bored to death with it, had one eye closed against the smoke. Apple, stopping, watched yearningly.

He found himself marching forward. What's this? he wondered. He hoped he wasn't going to ask the man for a cigarette. Of course he wasn't, he argued irritably. He had more sense and willpower than to do anything as stupid as that.

Apple brought the groundsman to a halt with, "Would you have a cigarette about you, please?"

He stood there in a stoop of shocked anguish and hungry anticipation as the man went through the slow, slow motions of putting down the hose, patting his pockets, getting out a crumpled packet and fumbling it open. After handing a cigarette over, he took the butt from his mouth and offered it for a light, coughing.

Staying aloof from the furious argument that was going on inside him, Apple lit up. He closed his eyes in love as the smoke went down deep into his lungs. On the exhale he whined with the joy of it all; and he bowed as he handed back the butt.

Glancing behind, Apple trotted across to the trees. He hid behind a broad trunk and took another drag of bliss. After doing so, he lifted his head to gaze dreamily at the sky.

He looked down. He glared. His joy fled. His upper body jerked as a huge belch surged up and violently out. Next, he was on his hands and knees, vomiting. His stomach blared pain. He was coated with an icy sweat. He felt terminally ill.

Well at least, Apple thought wretchedly, I know now what the blue pills are for.

And in that house in Wembley, the one with the drunken neighbours who had six screaming brats, there was a wife. She had broad, hefty shoulders, a square jaw and the beginnings of a moustache. Her hands were large, folding up to fists like horses' hooves. She snored. Her cooking was atrocious and she refused to wash dishes. That was her husband's job. He did it every night, meekly, wearing an apron which bore on the front the word *Its*.

Apple was musing this way the following evening, while circling the same cluster of trees. He had recovered from his nausea, though he hadn't lost his craving for tobacco. As he jogged, he chewed a piece of straw.

Apple's day, with one exception, had been a repeat of the day before, with again no appearance of June in the gym, another seven and a half laps with Philip (result the same), more instruction in the final fling. The exception was that a blue pill had not been taken; it was hidden behind the lining in his overnight bag, where it would be joined by others, one every morning.

Past the trees now, Apple left Wembley and Angus Watkin's domestic misery. After a glance behind—seeing nothing of Bill Burton—he set off at a brisk lope across the lawn. Two minutes brought him to the woodland patch.

From inside the cover of the trees, he looked back. Still no Burton. Grinning, Apple went on. He weaved quickly in and out of trunks, touching each one in passing as if playing a game. He had the glee of a boy on an escapade.

The woods thinned in time to an occasional tree. Apple ran at a good speed. His lungs were fine. He felt as though he could go on like this forever. He spat out the piece of straw.

The boundary hedge came into view. It was a pathetic thing. It looked to have been charged over by a regiment of soldiers in full pack. No toddler would have been delayed by it for more than a few seconds—though warning bells would have been set ringing in a room at the top of Damian House.

Apple took the hedge at a flying leap. He went on at the same easy, ground-eating pace that needed little effort. Feeling kind, he gave Watkin's wife a hairless upper lip.

Soon, rooftops and chimneys appeared. Apple began to circle. He was aiming to arrive behind the village inn. He had no firm plan in mind. Vaguely he expected to be able to find June without any trouble. This suited his mood.

Even so, Apple was surprised when he saw the track-suited figure ahead. It was June, jogging around the field that lay behind the pub.

Apple slowed. He went the rest of the way at a stooping walk, his legs bent and his trunk almost horizontal. From that position, aided by dry-stone walls, he could see neither the inn nor June.

He reached the wall ahead and peered over it. June was on the far side of the field. When she had circled and nearly drawn level, Apple raised his head higher and said, "Psst!"

June halted with a jolt, her eyes wide with startlement. Then she laughed and brought her hands together in a clapping clasp. "As someone or another once said: Christ, it's you."

"I guess it is."

"We sound like a couple of spies exchanging signals."

"Yes, but you've got it wrong. After the opening you asked if I was okay."

"And you told me you knew how to land," June said. She looked toward the inn. Apple stood taller to do the same. On a patch of lawn, in a deck chair, sat a man in purple slacks and a rainbow-coloured shirt. He had grey hair and wore sunglasses with mirror lenses.

"My Control," June said. "Keep down. Come on." She turned and jogged off, heading away from the pub. Apple followed crouchingly on his own side of the wall, which, at the corner, grew into the side of a ruined stone-built stable. He was straightening as June came around the building.

She said, "You're crazy to do this. I'm crazier to go along with it. But here you are so let's stroll." She added, as Apple glanced back, "He won't miss me for a while. I often drift away."

They ambled under the muscular arms of an oak tree. Apple decided against mentioning that the largest oak in the British Isles was in Scotland and reached a height of a hundred and fifty feet. He couldn't see how it would help.

"It shouldn't surprise you, me showing up," Apple said. "You seemed sure we'd meet again. You said as much."

"Not like this. I meant at Liverpool. The track meet."

"It's really on, then?"

"Of course," June said, looking up at him. "Don't you ever read the sports pages?"

The newspapers were in the hall, which he avoided. "What I mean is, will I really be running there in the three-thousand-metres race? I have my doubts."

"Leave them, Russ. You'll be running the three, and I, as Marcia Greystone-Cairn, will be running the mile. Don't your people tell you anything?"

"You've met Watkin," Apple said. "You can imagine what it's like to work under him." He went on to tell with enjoyable dislike of his chief's devious ways.

June nodded. "I know the type. Their slogan is, Never let your left hand know what that same left hand is doing, but tell the right one because you've got to have *something* to brag of your talent to."

"Yes. That's old Angus in a nutshell."

"We have plenty like that."

Apple said, "So I'm in the dark. I wish I knew what was going on."

"That's a question, Russ."

"Of course it is. Sorry."

"But look," June said. "I can tell you what most people seem to know. At least, on my side. Okay?"

"I'd be grateful."

"We'll be running at Liverpool in the British finals. We won't win, of course. But the aim is to come in second. That way we'll be going to Paris with the team as replacements."

"Paris?" Apple asked, trying not to look too taken aback.

"The East-West Games. Three days of track and field. It's a week after the Liverpool deal. That's all I can tell you."

"I know. Orders, orders."

June said, "It's not only that. My Control's a good guy and I wouldn't want to let him down. In any case, there's not much more I know about the operation. I'm only a minor cog."

"So am I," Apple said, thinking he wouldn't pursue the matter and liking June's loyalty. For the moment he was content to be taking this stroll with her. He asked about her background.

Small-town New York, she said. State college. A B.A. in semantics. A year with the city police, two with the FBI, the past three years with the Central Intelligence Agency. She told about some of her service experiences. She ended, "And athletics all along the way. I used to be pretty hot, but I hit my peak at twenty-one."

"But you're not worried about Liverpool?"

"No," June said shortly. "Now it's your turn, Russ."

Apple talked about himself. His service life sounded pallid in comparison with June's adventures. He wanted to make a good impression. Also, he wanted to offer something, in the form of a gift, as evidence of his interest. His liking for the girl had increased greatly.

"The night before I came to Damian House," he said, "I had a curious experience." He went on to impress and give his gift— the story of being attacked by Coveralls and Green-suit. He made it more dramatic and violent, as well as making the men huge.

June's response was disappointing. She asked, "Did you report it?"

"Well, no. I've told no one but you."

"Thanks for that," she said, smiling briefly. "But you ought to have given it to Watkin."

"I'm sure they were just a couple of muggers."

"Maybe so. Or there's another possibility, one you didn't have on your list."

"I think I covered them all."

"You'd been announced as a runner at Liverpool that same day," June said. "The toughs could have been working for another competitor in the three thousand. A rival."

Apple stopped walking. He asked, "Are you serious?"

June came back and stood in front of him. "Sure. There are times when there's not a lot of sportsmanship in sports, in case you didn't know."

He shook his head slowly, doubtingly. "I didn't."

June smiled. "Russ, you're one of the world's innocents."

Apple was furious to find that he was starting to blush. He quickly thought blowtorch, blowtorch, but the blush thrived as it spread across his face.

June tilted her head. "You want to know something else?" she said, her eyes earnest. "You're a real sweet guy."

No more able to take a direct compliment with panache than any other Englishman, Apple flickered a smile and felt his face growing redder and hotter.

"Must get back," June said. She stretched up, kissed his cheek, turned, and jogged away. She called back, "See you in Beatlesville."

The following days moved swiftly. Every morning Apple dutifully took a blue pill—took it from the bottle to his case. He trained, napped, ate well, absorbed the history of athletics. He was under the constant surveillance of a dozy-looking Bill Burton, who had made no mention of his charge's forty-five-minute absence while jogging. Apple thought of June, cigarettes, and Liverpool.

Apple now had the operation figured out. He didn't need to win the three thousand metres, only to get second place, and should he come third, could be the man who came second would be persuaded to catch a disease. The race was fairly in the bag.

He would go to Paris as emergency replacement. It was unlikely that he would do any running. All that was required of him was his presence, with a legitimate reason for being there. Also owning a sound, checkable reason would be the Red informant. He would need it doubly because at the athletes' village and at the stadium security would be tight—as it had been at all such meets since the Olympic Games in Munich. The Red would be a sports pressman with *Pravda*, or connected with Russian radio, or be with a Russian television crew. He would pass over papers, tapes, or possibly newsreel material.

Everything was set and looked good, Apple repeatedly mused. All he had to do was perform well in the three thousand, against the top runners from among a population of sixty million. Whenever he thought of it, Apple fumbled to get out his matches or stooped to snatch up a blade of grass.

On his last evening at Damian House, Apple found Giles Parker alone at the track. Nor was there to be a taking of the seven and a half laps. The two men ambled along on the cinders.

"Well, Porter," Parker said, "I've taught you what I possibly could in the time allotted to me."

"I've learned a great deal, sir. Thank you. I'm grateful."

"It's my job. Not a terribly exciting one, but it does have its compensations. I should like to hear that you did well in the coming race."

"I'll try my best, sir."

"You'll be running on asphalt, not cinder, which you'll find a lot easier. The choice of this place was deliberate. It's the same principle as wading a racehorse along the beach."

"Then I'll make better time than I did here."

"You will. But bear my instructions in mind." Giles Parker went on to give another of his lectures. After that he said, "I won't be there to see the race, unfortunately."

"They keep you pretty busy, sir, I imagine."

"No, it's not that. There's always the outside chance of someone from behind the Curtain being in the crowd or somewhere around. So I can't go." He made a vague gesture with his left hand, the one with the missing fingers. "I'm known to the other side."

Quietly, Apple said, "I see, sir." He felt chilled. However, he told himself that his imagination was leaping to conclusions, as it was apt to do in all matters connected with espionage. The trainer, à la Bill Burton and his scar, had probably lost the two fingers in an innocuous accident.

Giles Parker stopped and put out his good hand. "Best of luck to you, Porter."

Accepting and returning the iron-like shake, Apple said, "Thank you, sir. And you didn't quite manage to make me dislike you."

The trainer smiled. "No, but there's always another time."

"If you're ever passing Liverpool," Bill Burton said, glancing around from the wheel of the Rover, "keep passing."

"I see what you mean."

The streets were as forlorn as Christmas decorations in a garbage can. The scene was worsened by a slate-coloured sky that threatened rain. Like any other dockland/industrial city, here it was business all the way, with no frivolities such as trees and colour, or clothing that wasn't strictly utilitarian. The only signs of leisure were the unemployed, who leaned on walls as if they were rich friends.

It was early afternoon. At the stadium, Apple had learned from Burton during the long drive, some of the heats and other individual events had taken place in the morning. There would be no heats for the longer races, those of a mile and over, for exerting such energy twice in one day was out of the question. In any case, there were only fourteen entrants for the three thousand metres, a manageable number in an event that needed neither separate lanes nor starting blocks.

"So," Apple said now, tapping a matchstick on his thumbnail, "I'm the Southern Area champ, eh?"

"Which is neat considering that there's no such precise region, except in amateur boxing. Was not, I should say. It was created four weeks ago."

"How very convenient. And I suppose that a month from now it will be dropped."

"Don't ask me," Bill Burton said. "I don't know anything. I don't even know if there's a bar in this glamour spot we're going to. And there she is."

Looking at the gaunt back of the stadium that rose above the roofs of terrace houses, Apple mused that the reason for his late arrival, when all other athletes would have been here since morning, was to keep him under light wraps, away from nosy rivals. But he was musing this with indifference.

Apple put the matchstick between his teeth and chewed quickly. He was less sure of himself than before. He was also less sure of June, as regards performance. Her peak was long past, she had said. What if she failed and he won, or she won and he failed, or what if they both failed? There'd be no Paris. They would never meet again.

Apple realised he was not acting like a professional. He was letting a personal relationship interfere with his thinking on the operation. That, of course, as he knew, was why intramural associations were discouraged or taboo, depending on the circumstances. Although he had to admit that it made excellent sense, that didn't stop him from hoping for the best from what seemed to be a developing relationship with June—*if* they both got to Paris.

Bill Burton steered into the stadium's vast parking grounds. "Until further notice, Thirty-four," he said, "I don't know you're on earth."

"Check, Twenty-nine."

He stopped the Rover in a lane between parked cars. "See you around."

Half an hour later, Apple was alone in a long, bleak changing room that smelt of armpits and hairy combs. The stragglers who had been here when he came in had gone. Having changed, Apple wore underneath his track suit running shorts and a singlet, both blue and bearing the initial of the Civil Service Harriers.

He looked up from tying his shoelaces as the door opened. The man who came in was short and fat, fifty and bald and pink. His blazer pocket bore the badge of an amateur athletic association. He looked corpulently unhealthy; looked as if two push-ups would give him a cardiac seizure.

"You'll be Porter," he said, coming over. "The dark horse. I'm Percival Reed, head coach. How do you do."

Apple crouched up to shake hands. "Hello, Mr. Reed."

"We thought you weren't going to turn up. We thought that

perhaps you didn't even exist." He laughed to show it was a joke, the while patting his badge as if to demonstrate that his position allowed him to be jocular about the grave matter of sports.

"I was delayed. A lot of traffic."

Solemn again, Percival Reed asked, "What was your time in your last three thousand, Mr. Porter?"

Apple finished tying his shoelace. He looked up with, "Sorry. My mind's a blank. I'm always like this before a race. Stage-fright. You know how it is."

"Yes. The nerves can get a bit shredded. But surely you can tell me your average time."

Apple cocked his head. "What's that noise?" There was nothing to be heard except Reed's fat-man breathing.

"I don't hear anything."

"Sounded like the crowd getting worked up."

Percival Reed swept his arm around to expose the three watches on his wrist. "Possibly. The mile's due to start. It's actually the fifteen hundred metres, but we still call it the mile."

"I'd like to see it," Apple said, getting up.

"Yes, we have a good crop of girls this year."

Apple perked. "It's the *women's* mile?"

"That's right."

Apple moved swiftly toward the door. Halfway there he turned and shot back. "Nice to meet you, sir. Excuse me." He shot off again and left the changing room.

There was a long corridor lined with concrete. Apple chased along it to a four-way junction. He chose left. It seemed to have been the correct choice: he could hear the crowd somewhere above.

At another junction Apple went left again. The noise stayed the same. He ran faster. There were more turnings. He felt as if he were lost in a maze.

Flying around yet another corner, Apple narrowly avoided

crashing into Percival Reed, who was coming out of a door. Apple recognised the door as belonging to the dressing room. He had made a full circle.

"Which way?" he snapped. "Please."

Reed pointed a fat arm. "Straight on, straight on." He called after Apple as he ran off, "Conserve your strength!"

At the end of the concrete tunnel there was a flight of steps. The crowd's roar was louder. As Apple leapt upwards, he heard the crack of a pistol shot.

At the top of the stairway he came out into the wide, cavernous, open-ended entrance to the field. Scores of people were blocking the way to the track. But Apple didn't need to push through to see. It occurred to him as he stood at the back of the crush how beneficial his height was proving lately.

He saw the runners. They were approaching on the left, all fairly close together in a single-file line. June was lying third. Her head was up, her features were severe. There was not a dimple in sight.

The pack flew past. Slowly, it began to stretch, the spaces between girls growing larger. Although the positioning didn't change, June was being left behind. Apple clenched his fists.

When the outstrung pack passed again, he cupped both hands to his mouth and bellowed, "Paris!" It made no difference to him that he wouldn't be heard among the general clamour.

The bell rang for the final lap. Apple shook his clenched hands in rhythm with his nodding head. In some strange way it seemed to help. June was closing the gap.

Moving beautifully, she crept up on the girl in number two place, leaving the others behind. She narrowed the gap still more. Next, she was running at the side of number two. She stayed there.

"Get in front or behind," Apple groaned loudly. "You're giving yourself more distance. Think Paris."

The two girls, keeping side by side, were closing in on the leader, who kept glancing back. They were so close together they appeared to be trying to elbow each other off-balance.

Gradually they shifted into the next lane—Apple again groaning—as they moved closer to the girl in front. Then they drew level. The three ran in a line. They stayed like that over the last fifty yards and seemed to cross the finish line together.

Apple sagged. He heard a nearby man say, "Lousy time. Our girls are going to be churned into mincemeat in Paris."

Apple asked, "Who won?"

"Elling, I should think. She's the best."

Loudspeakers crackled. The announcer boomed, "Here is the result of the women's fifteen hundred metres. First, Marcia Greystone-Cairn, with a time of . . ."

With thirteen other men, Apple was sitting on the grass, near the starting line. They were waiting out the end of the high jump. No one was talking to anyone else. The thirteen sipped occasionally from their cans of glucose-loaded orange juice.

Apple hadn't even had a taste from his can, which had been handed to him by a uniformed official. Orange juice always went sour in his stomach and the aftertaste lasted for hours.

Apple was thinking about Paris. He could see himself strolling hand-in-hand with June along an elegant boulevard.

"Well well well," a hearty voice said. "Look at those initials. The good old CSH. How's tricks with the Harriers?"

Apple looked up to see a man in a crumpled suit. He carried a camera and had a card on his lapel that said PRESS. Thirty-ish, he had lank brown hair, uneven teeth, an ordinary face with a sallow complexion.

"Fine," Apple said.

The man lowered himself to a squat. Putting his hand over

68

the can of juice to move it out of the way, he said, "I used to be a member up till a couple of years ago."

"That's interesting."

"How's old Jim Beard?"

Apple raised his eyebrows. "Jim Beard of 17 March Road, telephone number eighty-two seventy-two ninety-four, husband of Lindy, whose leg is mending nicely after the car accident, father of George, who has just broken off his engagement to the Australian girl, that same Jim Beard is as well as can be expected for someone with a bronchial condition as severe as his."

No longer smiling, the man looked down. He asked a flat, "And Harry Tyler?"

"Taylor," Apple said. "Harold Taylor of Victory Mews, who won forty-two thousand pounds on the football pools last year, has bought himself a new Jaguar, white with red upholstery. He feels ten years younger than his sixty, and is happily fending off the attentions of three women. Their names are . . ."

After two minutes more of this, the man raised a cool hand. "Okay, okay. Very funny."

"I'm a regular card."

"So long, Thirty-four," the man said, rising, a sneer on his sallow face. He strolled off.

Apple lay back cheerfully on the grass. He had passed the memory test with colours battering in the breeze. Now all he needed to do was place well in the race. But he wasn't going to think about that.

Apple went back to Paris and June. He decided that on the whole it was better that her name wasn't April.

Activity around him roused Apple from his reverie. He sat up. The other men were getting out of their track suits. Apple began to do the same. He also began to feel nervous.

In five minutes, the loudspeakers booming, Apple and the thirteen runners were standing shoulder to shoulder, the right foot of each toeing the white line. Apple had a bad position, second to the outside, near the starter. He was thinking of that when the gun went off.

Apple's nerves shrieked. The gun, he realised as he careened forward from a spasmodic jerk, was a factor that ought to have been taken into consideration during training. The force of the explosion had been unexpected.

This Apple forgot on realising something else. He had made a bad mistake. He was out in front, alone.

Never lead, Giles Parker had drummed into him. Always let someone else do the pacing—unless you're lucky enough to have a clock in your head.

It was too late to fall back, Apple concluded. He would simply have to make the best of it. He was going to get to Paris if it killed him.

With the roar of the crowd in his ears, Apple kept up the pace. He found to his meliorating satisfaction that what Parker had said was true: running on asphalt was easier. There was no give underfoot. His shoes pounded down hard and pushed him on.

Apple was still in front after the first lap, the second, the third, and the fourth. He glanced back. The field was strung out, with a bunch trailing far behind, and three men close together some six yards back.

Apple ran as coached: hands slicing, head up and still, legs straight. After the fifth lap he looked behind. The six yards had become four.

Even while wailing to himself that it was too soon, far too soon, Apple poured on the pressure. Above the crowd's noise he could hear, faintly, the patter of footfalls from behind. He didn't look back again.

The patter had grown into a pounding by the time Apple was nearing the point of the final lap. He could feel one man right at his back. He wondered if his heels were going to be trodden on.

The bell clanged.

Apple couldn't give any more. He had used up the store of energy that he should have saved for the last spurt. His lungs and legs were paining. His ribs ached.

The pounding from behind grew louder. In the corner of his right eye, Apple saw flat hands flash in and out of view. Next appeared forearms. Next, the whole body.

Teeth bared, the man came on. Inch by inch he drew up until he was level. Apple tried. He tried his hardest. But he was unable to make any more speed. He felt, in fact, as if he were slowing, though that could have been due to the effect of the other man slowly drawing ahead.

There was a hundred yards to go to the finish line. Apple felt that he wouldn't even be able to get there, let alone claim back the lead from the man who had battled two or three feet on.

And now Apple heard more pounding from behind. He glared at the finish line to draw it closer, and put his body on the torture rack. His lungs seemed to be fighting his heart.

Hands appeared in the edge of his vision. There was nothing he could do except keep up the torture. But the line was close, and the forearms were slow in coming into view.

Forty yards, thirty, twenty, ten. The man was almost level. The leader, with four yards to spare, flashed across the line.

Apple felt only the jolt, not the pain, as an elbow crashed into his biceps. If that had been a foul, it had a reverse effect: the man at his side ebbed. He was several inches behind as Apple went across the finish line at an agonizing slog.

Apple had placed second.

He made himself keep going, but at a slumping lope. Never stop suddenly, Giles Parker had warned; your heart might stop with you.

When Apple did let his legs end their action, he stood in a hunch, hands pressed to the back of his hips in the untaught, instinctive pose that helped the lungs of spent runners and asthmatics. Save for his pride, he would have sunk to a kneel. His legs had palsy.

Apple was distantly, dizzily aware of shaking several hands, of the loudspeakers giving their nasal booming, of ambling back to where he had left his track suit. He put it on, though how he found the energy to do so, he didn't know. If he hadn't known how easy it was to catch cold after a run, he would have left the stifling suit off.

The other men had already dressed and gone. Apple caught up with them in the vast entryway. Only now, recovering, was he beginning to feel the elation of success. This increased when, among the scores of athletes surrounding the runners, he saw June.

She came over to him with a loud, "Jolly well done."

"Thanks. You too. Congratulations, Miss Greystone-Cairn."

She gave his hand a forthright shake. In an undertone, accent changed, she said, "These people are damn good, Russ."

"I know. And I know what went wrong. I didn't drink my orange juice. There was probably a booster in it."

June shook her head. "Good old innocent you."

"Eh?" Apple said.

"Our drinks were clean, Russ. It's the others who had spiked drinks. Just enough to take the edge off their drive and their determination. We were lucky to place. These people could've run us into the ground, and they nearly did."

"Oh," Apple said.

CHAPTER 3

The train rattled through open country. What ought to have been a pretty, representational picture of the English landscape was made into a wobbly abstract work by the rain lashing against the window.

Apple didn't mind. For one thing, he felt rich with the satisfaction of his success. For another, being in the corner by the window allowed him to keep fairly aloof from the others in the carriage. Their boisterousness made him feel old.

The other passengers, in their late teens or early twenties, were all among the southbound of those who had competed at Liverpool; and all, by their talk and manner, were due to appear in Paris in a week's time. They glowed with health and victory, talked non-stop, went constantly out of the carriage and returned with odds and ends of gossip from further along the corridor. Apple chewed steadily on a matchstick.

Yesterday, in the changing room, reporters had been allowed in. One of the men was the agent who had pumped about the Harriers. He told Apple quietly, "There's a reservation for you at the Royal Duke Hotel. Go there straight from here. In the morning, be on the ten o'clock train for London, in section four."

"Where is this hotel?"

"The Royal Duke, with two hundred bedrooms, high-speed lifts and a French chef, with a garage underneath and a helicopter pad on the roof? Oh, I think you'll manage to find it, Thirty-four."

"Too, too kind."

"My name's Forty-one, by the way. So long."

Apple was treating himself to a new matchstick when yet again the carriage door slid open. The young man who leaned in was twitching with excitement. "Guess what?" he asked. "Guess bloody what?"

When the chorus of whats had died down, he said, teasing like a raconteur, "You'll never guess what's just happened to Joe Ross. I can't believe it."

Apple leaned forward. Joe Ross was the runner who had beaten him in the three thousand.

Surviving the verbal assault, the raconteur said, nodding seriously, "Some great elephant of a man stepped on Joe's foot. It's hurting like hell and might have a broken bone. He might be out of the Paris deal."

While exclaiming, everyone turned to look at Apple. With an apologetic smile, he leaned back into his corner. He shrugged when someone said, "Looks good for you."

Accidents, he thought, would happen, and this one might be a minor affair, a bruise. But naturally he was going to assume that it was no accident at all.

Talk in the carriage switched to other matters among the comings and goings. Apple was inattentive, wistful with his match, until he caught the mention of a familiar name.

He asked, "What was that about the mile?"

The girl across from him said, "Greystone-Cairn. She's not a bit friendly. Got herself stuck back there all alone. Some people do put on the touch-me-not rubbish when they've had a win."

"You mean she's on this train?"

"Yes," someone else said. "She lives in London, I've heard. The stuck-up bitch."

The door trundled open again. This time the doorway was blocked by three men who appeared to be playing the part of reporters in a stage farce. They had shabby raincoats and back-tilted hats. They all talked at once, the while looking at Apple.

He gathered from the jabber that they wanted to interview him, as there was a chance that he would be representing Britain in the East-West Games. One man said, "The doc's had a look at that foot of Ross's and thinks a broken bone is a distinct possibility. It'll have to be X-rayed."

The reporters were eased aside. Another man looked into the carriage. He was agent Forty-one, and apparently still using the press cover. He said, "Sorry, boys. Mr. Porter promised me an interview yesterday. I've been trying to find him. On this train, it's like looking for a needle in a haystack." He pronounced the last word heavily. "So, Mr. Porter, shall we wander along to the bar and have a natter?"

Apple got up. "Yes, I suppose so."

He moved past the grumbling reporters, whom Forty-one told, "Don't worry, he won't jump out. It'll be your turn after me."

Apple followed him along the corridor. Around a bend, Forty-one looked behind with a wink and, "There's someone back here would like to see you."

Apple smiled. "Really?"

"By the way, you were told to be in section four."

"I didn't forget. That part, it so happens, is for smokers." The mistake, like the matter of the starting-pistol, Apple had smoothed over in his mind. He liked to believe that every detail, down to the most minor, was studiously taken care of in the world of espionage. He felt less vulnerable that way.

Forty-one stopped at a private compartment. He tapped, opened the door, and ushered Apple inside. Apple said a dull, disappointed, "Good morning, sir."

"I might as well tell you," Angus Watkin said, lifting the cozy off the teapot, "that I know about your romantic escapade the other night in Little Wentworth."

"Ah," Apple said. He felt more uncomfortable than he would have normally because of being in the minute compartment. Confined spaces gave him claustrophobia. Looking across the table at his chief, he added, "I can explain."

"I didn't get it from Burton, by the by. He doesn't even know that it happened, and I see no reason why he should be told. It would do his pride no good."

As always whenever Watkin showed a hint of being human, Apple experienced a prickle of annoyance. He asked, "It came from the Mayflower end, sir?"

"No. The report came through one of Damian House's boundary patrol guards."

"I didn't know there were any."

"Only at certain times," Angus Watkin said, pouring tea. "And I imagine, Porter, that they don't exactly make themselves obvious."

"I'd like to explain, sir, that my trip to Little Wentworth wasn't romantic. Not in the least."

"Explain away."

"One day I saw the CIA girl wandering around at Damian House. I thought that a bit peculiar. So I went over to the village to nose about a bit. I met the girl. We talked, and I believe that everything is straight."

"That's awfully nice to know," Watkin said heavily. "I can't tell you how relieved I am."

"Yes, sir," Apple mumbled, hating rampantly. He accepted the cup that was slid across to him.

His chief signalled that the matter was closed, if not forgotten, and the explanation accepted as a lie, by saying, "There's only one organisation that makes worse tea than British Rail, and that's Naval Intelligence. With them, it's probably a form of sadism. The lash and keel-hauling have been made illegal, I understand."

As he knew that his superior was trying to be funny, Apple performed a smile. He sipped his tea. Watkin tasted his with a spoon, and left it at that. He said, "I shall be alighting at the next station, near which I hope to find a decent restaurant. You, Porter, after meeting the gentleman in quotes of the press, will return here, and stay here, in company with Forty-one. Clear?"

"Yes, sir," Apple said, thinking, In other words, no June.

Watkin folded his arms in a businesslike manner. "Now to the nub. The coming operation. What you need to know at the moment is that the man you will be meeting in Paris really belongs to the Americans. We shall call him Igor for the time being. He has been selling information to the Central Intelligence Agency for years. But he tends to be somewhat of a prima donna, because of which he has taken a dislike to his normal contact. Time being a factor, the Americans were unable to arrange for a suitable substitute, one with all the required qualifications. Therefore we were brought into the picture. Are you following, Porter?"

Apple stopped patting the pocket wherein lay his matchbox. "Yes, sir, I am. Acutely."

"Don't let your tea get cold."

Apple obediently gulped at the weak liquid that had a vague flavour of coffee. As he put the cup down, Watkin went on.

"Igor has an A-1 security rating with the KGB. Therefore he is always able to come through to the West. He has no desire to stay on this side. His life in Moscow is rich. He has an apartment all to himself, a rare luxury in Russia. His interest in politics is nil and he is in the information business strictly for the cash. He would probably sell his mother if the price was right. He is a playboy, a womaniser. For which pastime he needs a constant flow of ready cash."

Apple nodded. He was faintly disturbed to find that he felt envious of Igor.

"This time," Angus Watkin said, "we will do the pick-up, the Americans will pay, and the information will be shared. It's not an unusual arrangement, and after all, we did steer Igor to the CIA in the first place. Does all that, Porter, satisfactorily explain to you the presence of the young lady with the odd accent?"

"Yes, sir, it does."

"So we can now stop being interested in her, can't we?"

"Certainly, sir."

Angus Watkin glanced with dislike at the window's streaky green abstract. "But back to Igor. He is, as I have said, temperamental. He has power, and knows it, and you are aware of what possession of power can do to certain types of people."

Apple said a deadpan, "I think I am, sir."

"Therefore you will need to talk to him in a subservient fashion and treat him with gloves of the finest velvet. If you should happen to rub him the wrong way—there goes the operation."

"I shall handle Igor with the greatest of care, sir."

"Good," Watkin said. "I'm telling you all this now for two reasons. One, to set you right on the American involvement. Two, so there will be less for you to have to absorb on your final briefing."

"I understand, sir," Apple said, but he was wondering about

those qualifications. June could run. She could speak Russian well enough. Why hadn't she been used by the CIA?

Angus Watkin looked at his watch. He said, "As to the following week. I want you to run morning and evening, take a lot of rest, stay home at nights and go to bed early, and keep to the same diet that you were on at Damian House. If you can't manage the cooking yourself, find a restaurant that will oblige. The expense will be refunded to you."

"I'll probably do a bit of each, cooking and eating out."

"And don't forget your blue pill. You have, I hope, been taking it regularly."

Apple said sincerely, honestly, "The first thing I do after waking up every morning, sir, is reach for that bottle."

"Excellent," Watkin said. He lifted the teapot. There was definite relish in the movement, if not in his face or his voice, as he said, "Let me give you some more tea, Porter."

The Bloomsbury flat was comfortable. It had large rooms whose high ceilings wore sculpted plaster, pseudo-Edwardian furniture to go with the decor, stout walls, and central heating. The tall windows looked down onto a pleasant street, and from one window there was a view of a back corner of the British Museum.

On the morning after his return from Liverpool, Apple came home from an early run, luxuriated through a long shower, dried himself, and put on his robe. This garment was coloured in screaming reds, greens, and blues; the squares of the plaid pattern measured a foot each way.

Feeling, as always, smugly outrageous in his robe, and with his hair wet and tangly, Apple went barefoot to the kitchen to have breakfast.

The haddock he had left, pre-run, in the oven to poach was ready. He followed that with another diet item, a pair of soft-boiled eggs eaten with whole-meal bread, and finished with the third, a large glass of goat's milk.

Orders having been followed, Apple next fixed his favourite food: toast with lemon marmalade. Crunching happily at the kitchen table, he opened the newspaper that he had brought up with him from the mail table in the hall downstairs.

The paper he had read at the Liverpool hotel had merely listed his name on the rear page that was devoted to the track meet. In today's, he was given a whole two inches, underneath a photograph that was nearly recognisable, both underneath a large piece on the winner of the three thousand metres. Joe Ross had suffered a foot injury while returning home to Brighton and his appearance in Paris was now in doubt. Second X rays were being taken in Harley Street.

The copy on Apple said that he was a possible for the East-West Games, depending on Ross's injury. He was unknown in sporting circles and, at the age of twenty-eight, seemed too old for a gruelling test such as the three thousand. The item said between its lines that the country would be served best in Paris if Joe Ross proved fit.

Apple was disinterested. He gave more time to the brief profile, with photograph, on the winner of the mile, Miss Marcia Greystone-Cairn, who had been living in South Africa until recently. He clipped the picture out and pinned it on the kitchen door.

Later, dressed in his normal everyday clothes, Apple left the flat, went down three flights of stairs and out to the street. Signalling the first vacant cab that came along, he got in. The expense he excused by telling himself that he was, after all, on vacation.

It seemed odd, arriving at the United Kingdom Philological Institute at mid-morning. It felt odd-awful, not pausing as usual at the foot of the marble staircase to light a cigarette. Apple went up swiftly.

When he entered Professor Warden's office, the old man looked up with a smile that would have been bright had it not been for the dullness of his dentures.

"Ah, Porter," he said. "The student of Basque."

"Yes, that's what I came to see you about, Professor."

Warden got up and came around his messy desk. He was a small man with white hair, a suit thirty years out of fashion, and a bemused manner. His thin, long-nosed face seemed to match his habit of blinking constantly.

Head tilted far back, smiling up, he accused, "You did not go to San Sebastian."

"No, sir, I didn't."

"One of the secretaries showed me a newspaper. *You* were in it, Porter. You've been to Liverpool. You're quite a good—um—um—"

"Runner?"

"No no no, an excellent—er—er—"

"Racer?"

Professor Warden shook his head. Although he spoke fourteen languages fluently, he was often unable to find the word he wanted in English. He changed his headshake to a nod, saying, "A good *fibber*, Porter. I believed your story."

"Well, it's like this," Apple began. He went on to explain his semi-secret membership in the Civil Service Harriers, his shyness, his conviction that he wasn't good enough for competition. "Friends talked me into it. I didn't want you to know because I was sure I'd be greatly outrun."

"But you weren't, my boy. You did spendidly. We're all so proud here at the UKPI. You must go and show yourself to the secretaries. Did I ever tell you about the time I ran in the Oxford and Cambridge—um—"

Continuing, when he had found the right word, to relate his try in the marathon, Professor Warden moved back to his chair. He picked up one of his pipes. There were six in a rack, all pre-packed. He flicked on a lighter and talked between puffs.

Apple backed away from the smoke, his mouth watering. He arrived by the window, which was partly open. Turning, he pushed it open more—and during the act caught a glimpse of movement along the street below.

Apple had a sensation of recognition. It lasted briefly. In giving his attention fully to the place of glimpse, he saw nothing. He didn't know what had caused the sensation. It could have been a familiar vehicle, or colour, or person. He did know that a prickling had passed over his scalp.

Am I being tailed? he wondered.

Apple spent another ten minutes with Professor Warden, five in the typing pool basking in the girls' admiration, and a final five being congratulated by colleagues. He left the building.

Walking, Apple found that he had no feeling of having a shadow, that coolness between the shoulder blades. Which, he mused, didn't necessarily mean that he wasn't being tailed, only that the tailer could be an expert. Experts watched a quarry's legs.

After covering several streets, with looks behind performed in the prescribed manner, Apple concluded that, not unusually, he was being melodramatic. There was no shadow. He went in search of a quality restaurant.

Lunch over, its bill kept for Accounts, Apple strolled home. There, he napped and later read. After jogging for two hours he prepared his own dinner, listened to classical tapes and went to bed at ten o'clock. His teeth ached with chewing matchsticks.

Except for his visit to the Institute, the next day was the same, as was the next, when Apple heard on the radio that Joe Ross's foot was free of damage and that he would be running in

Paris. The third day followed the pattern up until late afternoon.

The ringing of the telephone brought Apple from his bedroom, where he had been napping. Yawning his way to the living room, he picked up the receiver and chanted his number. A female voice said, "Christ, it's you."

Apple laughed, snapping alert. "Wonderful. I've just been dreaming about you."

"Respectably, I hope."

"My innocence has its limits," Apple said boldly, then took a hold on the wild inner man. "But how did you know where to call me?"

"A brilliant piece of deduction," June said. "I looked in the telephone book."

"Where are you? Never mind. I don't suppose you're allowed to mention that."

"Sorry. And I can't tell you where I do my training. Ah well. Did you hear about Ross?"

"Yes," Apple said. "Listen, we've got to meet. Tonight. Let's get together and have a meal."

"Russ, you're out of your mind."

"Watkin found out about Little Wentworth. He didn't exactly foam at the mouth. Go out jogging and we'll meet somewhere."

"Evenings I cycle. The streets aren't safe to be on foot, my Control says. Though he lets me cycle alone."

"Well, there you are. We're golden. I'll rent a bicycle and meet you." He went on to talk persuasively.

June said, "Gee, I don't know."

Wearing flannels, a blazer and an open-neck shirt, Apple walked into the rental and repair shop, which smelt of just-snuffed candles. He was heading for the row of hire bicycles

83

when his eye was caught by a Vespa. It was bright red, squat, and bulbous—a rogue's machine. Stopping, Apple smiled down at the scooter in temptation.

A voice at his side began to quote daily, weekly, and monthly terms, insurance included. Apple didn't take his rapt gaze off the Vespa. For all he was aware, the man beside him could have been the Hunchback of Notre Dame.

He asked, "How do you work these things?"

"Same as a motorbike. If you can ride one of them, you can ride one of these."

Ten minutes later, Apple was putt-putting away from the shop on the impertinent red scooter. That he stuck up from it like a cocktail stick in a cherry bothered him not at all. It was how he felt that mattered. He felt rakish. And he was going to meet June.

She was there first, waiting opposite the Odeon in Leicester Square. From the grey bundle tied on her bike's carrier, it was obvious that she had left base with a track suit over the colourful summer dress she wore now.

Spreading her arms as Apple came to a halt, June said, "You look fabulous. A knight in shining blazer."

"Only on the elbows. Hello. You look beautiful."

"We're losing what's left of our brains."

Apple shook his head. "No one's going to pull us out at this stage of the game."

"You're probably right."

"Shall we wine and dine?"

"Indeed we shall. Name the place."

"Follow me."

Once out of the West End, rush hour past, the streets were fairly quiet as to traffic. Apple kept the Vespa to tick-over speed so that June wouldn't have to labour to keep up. For fun, he made elaborate signals whenever he made a turn.

The restaurant, in Stepney, would have rated in a guide book as two bent forks. But it was large, bustly, and cheerful. The diners ranged from men in working clothes to merchants with ledgers to pore over, from women with babes at the breast to matrons collared in fur neckpieces. The food here was plain, good, and reasonable.

Following a waiter's jerked thumb, Apple and June found a table for two in the room's middle. They settled and shared a scan of the sauce-stained menu. Apple said, "The wining bit is out, I'm afraid. I've just remembered that this place isn't licenced."

"It's just as well. No point in us going completely nuts, breaking training. It'll be bad enough eating some of this beautiful sounding goo. Like yum."

"Anyway, I wouldn't be able to show off. I wouldn't know a good wine if it wore a dinner jacket."

"I once drank a whole bottle of rot-gut while trying to get this dope peddler wiped out. I was the one who got wiped. It was in Greenwich Village when . . ."

They swapped experiences throughout the meal. Apple exaggerated over the bean soup, borrowed with the tripe and onions, lied outright as a spice for the suet pudding. He forgave himself, his motives being the finest. June, he thought, was one of the best things that had ever happened to him.

They dared coffee. Stirring his cup, Apple asked, "How d'you think you'll do in Paris?"

"Listen," June said, "I don't think we ought to talk about the caper, do you?"

"Perhaps you're right. Yes, in fact, you are. And not for obvious reasons. We'll talk about us. Let's pretend that I'm a clerk and you're a secretary."

"You have a deal, Russ. But I can answer that one question, sure. In Paris, I'll do miserably. No one's going to be able to pass around spiked drinks at an international meet. I'll trail the field. Not that it matters."

"Of course not," Apple said, wishing either that they had candles on the table or that he wasn't a romantic.

"Another thing, Russ. If it's all the same to you, I'll be a millionairess who's playing at being a secretary because she's taken a fancy to this nice clerk from the shoestore."

Apple laughed while furiously thinking blowtorch. It worked: the blush stopped on his neck, receded. He said, "Right. And I'll be a prince of the Austro-Hungarian Empire who's fallen for this secretary, and he's afraid that if she finds out he's of the blood purple, she'll give him the push. She hates rank and wealth."

"Hey, now wait a minute."

For a while they joked back and forth. Then Apple was puzzled to see June reach toward his left, act as if picking something up. She took the pincered fingers to her mouth. Acting a chew, she asked, "How are you at lip-reading?" Her eyes were serious.

He said, "Fair."

June performed a swallow. Smiling, she leaned forward, elbows on the table. She rested her chin on the heels of her hands, thus cupping her mouth. It was an intimate, natural-looking pose.

In silence, June worked her lips carefully. They said, "There is a spook over against the wall. He is alone. To your right rear. He cannot see your face."

Apple asked quietly, "How d'you know he's a spook?"

"Takes one to know one. All the signs are right. He is here for our benefit. Between pretending to read a book, he has looked at everyone but us."

"Friend or foe?"

"That I cannot say," June's lips created. "I do not know him. Maybe you do. You can take a gander with routine eight."

"I don't know it."

With her eyes crinkled up as though she were smiling, June explained. When someone passed their table, she would talk to Apple urgently, pointing. He would turn to stare after the departing someone. The operative would be forced to do the same, to try and discover the reason for the acute interest. The moment he did, June would signal Apple, who would then have a fast look at the operative without him being aware of it.

"That way," June finished, "he will not tumble that we have tumbled."

"Good," Apple said. "The next person to go by. Meanwhile I'll pay the bill. Upstairs is standing us a treat."

June stayed in the same position. She talked to Apple in a normal way, about the food, while he tried to catch their waiter's eye. He hadn't yet succeeded when a woman went past, heading for the door.

June swooped forward across the table. Her eyes were dartingly alive as she pointed semi-covertly and jabbered gibberish. Apple turned. He stared at the woman's back. In a moment June hissed, "Now!" Apple glanced at the man. He didn't know him, had no sense of recognition.

Turning back to June, Apple said, "A stranger to me. But yes, I think you're right. He's one of the herd. A spook."

"What do we do now?"

"We pay the bill and get the hell out of here."

With the door clanging shut behind them, they crossed to the kerb. The night street was bright from the glaring orange-tone lamps high above, which made everything stark and grim. Passing cars were wasting power with their lights.

Apple and June crossed to the opposite side, where the bicycle stood leaning against the scooter. That gave Apple an idea—private, not professional. He said, "Let's see if we were right about Spooky. Come on. Into this shop doorway."

"Sure. If he comes out quickly, we'll know."

In the recessed entrance to the store they stood together a yard back from the front, seeable but not in the full glare. June said, "It'll look funny, us simply standing here. We'll give the tumble away."

Apple put his arm around her shoulders. "Not if we . . ."

June looked up at him as he drew her closer. "If we what? Oh, I see. You mean if we . . ."

The kiss lasted a long time. It was warm but reasonably chaste, intimate without being erotic, a statement of mutual attraction. Apple embraced June firmly, while she lazed her fingers in the hair at the back of his neck.

At the sound of a clang, they eased their faces apart and directed them across the street. The assumed operative had come out of the restaurant. In his mid-twenties, he had brown hair to go with the dullness of his slacks and tweed jacket and polo-neck sweater.

He stood in the centre of the pavement, from where he swept his eyes around casually. He was good. The hesitation was hardly perceptible as his gaze went by the doorway.

"A spook," Apple whispered.

June said softly, "Yes, and he's spotted us. So now what?"

"We can amble over and ask him what his game is, or we can flee into the night."

"Myself, I'm all for fleeing."

The man looked at his watch, giving the impression he was waiting for someone. He stood in an easy slouch. After patting his pockets, he brought out cigarettes.

Apple sighed, but his need made him recall a piece of business from Training Three. He whispered, "As soon as the flame gets near his face, we'll slip quietly to the bikes. He'll be purblinded for a few seconds."

"Cool, Russ."

"You go on at a running start. I'll follow. Check?"

"Check, Thirty-four."

The man across the street flicked on a light, which he raised to his cigarette.

On tiptoe, Apple and June left the doorway fast and went to the machines. June grabbed her bicycle and ran with it before jumping onto the saddle.

Apple pushed the Vespa from its prop. He switched on and kicked down on the starter pedal. The motor stayed dead. As he kicked again, he looked back. The man was walking the other way obliquely across the road.

The motor started. Sitting, Apple twisted the handle to produce power. The scooter jerked away. It soon caught up with June, who was pedalling at full pelt. Apple steered abreast of her on the outside.

He called, "I think he's got a car."

"That doesn't make us very safe."

"We don't know his intentions."

What June shouted in reply was drowned by the roar of a passing truck. Apple looked behind. He saw a car following. Even if it hadn't been a giveaway by being as bland as the man from the restaurant, the stark lighting showed clearly the identity of the driver.

"Here he comes," Apple shouted. "Hold my hand." He reached out.

"Are you kidding?"

"No. Give me your hand and I'll tow you."

"Right. You're a hotshot." She put out her arm.

Their hands fumbled together, made the clasp. Their arms became strainingly rigid as Apple put on speed, towing June along slightly to his rear. He glanced at her face. It was tense.

He yelled, "Scared?"

She nodded. "Petrified. Both of this and Spooky. But go faster if you want."

He went faster. They came up behind a dawdling lorry. Apple steered out to pass. An approaching car came within inches of the red scooter. Apple, while shuddering, smiled in case June was looking at him.

He called, "Be prepared to turn. The next street. We'll try and lose this guy."

"That we'll never do."

They came to a corner. Apple took it with little reduction in speed. The bright orange lighting was left behind. The street was residential, dim and quiet.

"Listen," Apple shouted, after glancing behind and seeing that the car was coming. "I'll tell you what we can try."

"Let me tell *you* something, Russ."

"What?"

"We don't have our lights on."

"Christ, so we don't." The way ahead was growing darker as they went further from the glow behind. "We can unclasp briefly and turn the switches."

"But lights'll make it easier for Spooky to see us. Let's take a chance on hitting a wall."

"Or on being stopped by a patrol car."

"Which might be a nice thing to happen," June shouted. "But what is it that we're going to try?"

Apple explained as he went along the street. Turning another corner, he said, "It'll work if Spooky stays the same distance back."

"And if we find the right situation."

Apple had been looking behind. Only now was the car coming into view, with its headlights down on dim. He turned, saying, "It'll work, I think."

For five minutes he drove as fast as he dared in the gloom of street after street, taking every corner that presented itself. At last he saw what he wanted. He passed the lone cyclist and made a quick circle of the block.

On the final corner he shouted, "Get ready!"

They turned the bend. Apple speeded up. He let go of June's hand. She went zooming across to the other side of the street. There, she swerved in a dangerous lean between two parked cars. Apple heard a crash, the unmistakable sound of a falling bicycle.

Looking back, he could see no sign of June, which meant that neither could the car's driver. Apple knew that June was all right; she would have rolled with the planned fall.

The nose of the car appeared—and Apple hadn't yet caught up to the man on the bicycle. He twisted the accelerator handle viciously. Squealing a protest at being abused, the scooter reared up and charged forward.

Apple stuck out his arm. He drew alongside the cyclist, braked to the same speed and shouted, "You dropped this."

The man looked around, blinked, let go of the handlebar and reached out. "What is it?"

Apple grabbed the hand. He set his machine going faster, towing the man, who yelled a squeaky, "Watcha doing?" He was forty, gaunt-faced, and wearing a raincoat.

"You've got to stop bothering my sister," Apple snarled. He hoped the car behind would keep its lights on dim. Since June had short hair, the gambit had a good chance of succeeding.

"Let go!" the man screamed as Apple went still faster. "You're going to kill me!" He was glaring straight ahead as if into a vision of hell. "What sister?"

"Our Maggie. She's sick of you being a nuisance."

"For God's sake. I don't know what you're on about."

"You're a bloody menace," Apple shouted. There was a four-way junction ahead. "If you bother our Maggie again, Jim Smith, you'll get worse than this."

"You've made a mistake," the man squealed, still glaring. "My name's not Smith."

"It isn't?"

"No!"

"Oh, then I've got the wrong man," Apple said. "Sorry about that." He let go of the hand and swept away across the road, curving into another street at the junction.

Speeding on, Apple glanced back. The cyclist was just going from view in the same direction as before. Apple turned back front to check for safety, then looked behind again.

The tail car was there. It had stopped in the middle of the crossroads. When Apple glanced back a third time, the car was swinging around to follow him.

He switched on the lights. Slowly, he built up to maximum speed in moving along the straight road. While he knew he couldn't outrun the car, he also knew that he had the advantage of having a smaller vehicle. That was going to turn the trick.

Traffic lights lay ahead. They showed green. Before Apple could get there, they flicked to yellow. They were red when he went flashing across. He threw a glance back. The car had also crashed the red.

Immediately after that, Apple saw what he needed. It was a narrow foot-passage between buildings. He slammed on his brakes. The Vespa yammered again and went into a skid. Apple managed to regain control. By then, he was exactly opposite the passage. He steered into it, smiling, and sped along with a foot of space on either side.

The following morning, after jogging, after breakfast, Apple returned the scooter and walked the rest of the way to Covent

Garden. He went into a mammoth clothing store. The appoint-
ment had been arranged in Liverpool.

When all the athletes had dressed, winners and stand-bys had
been called together by the head coach, Percival Reed. Rising on
his toes, he had said, "The Russians are insisting on building up
the Paris meet to a mini-Olympics. That's because they have
some really fine performers this year and want to get the greatest
possible promotion out of the occasion. They want a full-dress
parade to open the event and all the fanfare possible. No one's
enough against the idea to veto it, except our accountant, so you
are all going to be outfitted with uniforms."

Now, the same crowd was assembled when Apple walked into
the men's department. He nodded at and shook hands with
many among the forty-odd men. From Joe Ross he got a friendly
wave. Everyone was friendly save the clerks, who looked at
Apple with doubt and defence in their eyes.

The off-the-peg outfit had already been selected. It was pale
green slacks and shirt, dark green jacket and tie. There would be
no headgear, Apple gathered with relief; he hated hats and anything else that served to increase his height.

While waiting his turn for a try-on, Apple browsed away
from the main group, looking at jazzy clothing that his inner
man would have loved to sport but his outer shrank away from.
He became uncasual on seeing the sign. It said WOMEN'S DEPT
THIS WAY.

Of course, Apple thought.

He followed the arrows, which brought him to an arch,
though he need only have followed the noise. This shrill ca-
cophony rose from the female athletes who were milling around
the large area.

Even so, Apple might have gone through had it not been for
the matron floorwalker who stared at him coldly, as if he had
come to play Peeping Tom. He stayed in the arch and cast about
over the matron's head.

He and June saw each other at the same moment. After a pause, June turned the other way and moved to a clear patch. She stood in front of a mirror. She held the green jacket she was carrying against herself. Via her reflection, she again met Apple's eyes.

June lip-spoke, "Everything go okay last night?"

"Yes," he mouthed. "And you?"

"Yes. But I found out who Spooky was."

"Oh dear."

"Right. He was one of my people. I got a rocket from my Control. He was livid. I told him that we had met by accident. That only made him worse."

Apple worked his mouth in elaborate silence: "Maybe the Brits and the Mayflowers aren't as cozy as we think."

"I don't know. But anyway, the word on our meeting is sure to get to your people, if it has not already. I think you would be wise to tell them about it first, before they tell you."

"Good idea. I will do that."

June's lips formed, "I will try to call you later, to see how you got on. Though I might not be able to. I am being watched most of the time."

"Play it safe."

"Check. See you in Paris. Over and out." She turned away from the mirror and joined the other women.

Apple shortened his gaze. He twitched to find that he was being gaped at by the matron floorwalker, who obviously had been observing his whole mime performance. Returning her stare, Apple twisted and writhed his lips, the while leaning forward. Her own mouth in a strange shape, the woman began to back away.

Apple turned and left. He was delighted with himself for the fact that he hadn't had to think blowtorch. He wondered if he could be improving. It was only the thousandth time he had had this wonder.

An hour later Apple left the store with a bulky package. The dubious clerks had managed to fit him out by the lengthening of sleeves and trouser cuffs.

Walking, Apple experienced a brief visitation of that feeling between the shoulder blades. It could be a shadow, he thought, but it could also be the stares that often followed him. And if a tail it was, he had a nice selection to choose from—his own people, the CIA, a Hammer, and possibly an athletic rival. There was nothing like variety.

He went into a telephone box on a quiet street. It needed to be quiet because traffic noise would be a nuisance: Apple always kept booth doors open on account of his claustrophobia.

With his package used as a doorstop, Apple fed the coin slot and dialled Upstairs. The male voice that answered asked a casual, "Well?"

Apple said, "I'd like to talk to Mr. Haystack in room thirty-four, please."

"I think you've made a mistake, got the wrong place. What number did you dial?"

Apple quoted six digits. The first three belonged to himself, his standard number, the others identified the person he wanted to talk to. A long pause followed. The voice said at last, "Yes, that's right. Hold on, please." Angus Watkin was available.

He came on the line a moment later with, "Well, Porter?" It sounded weary, as though he and Apple had been talking for an hour.

"Sir, I think I ought to tell you that last night, by coincidence, I ran across the CIA female operative. I know that it probably doesn't matter in the slightest, but I thought I'd let you know anyway."

"How very sensible of you, Porter," Watkin said, in the tone an officer might use in telling the firing squad to take aim. "And just where, precisely, did this felicitous meeting take place?"

Apple told about borrowing a friend's scooter so that he could go out into the country for his evening run; about seeing the girl while cutting through Leicester Square; about going with her to dine because she happened to know of a restaurant that could serve exactly the type of meal he wanted for his training diet.

"Actually, sir, it ended up quite funnily, which was good after being in such boring company. These Americans are so tedious. You see, we got chased by a man in a car. He'd been ogling the girl in the restaurant. He had a face like a navel, intelligence showing nowhere. The girl and I split up quickly, and then I ran over a cat. Quite funny."

Angus Watkin gave two long, heavy sighs. "Porter," he said, "you lie like a cheap rug. You curl at the corners."

"But, sir, I—"

"Good-*bye*, Porter." The line went dead.

Apple grinned as he cradled the receiver. The meeting would do him no good, but it hadn't done him much harm. It couldn't, not at this stage of the operation.

Before picking up his parcel to leave, Apple brought out one of his two matchboxes and pampered himself with ritual.

After leaving the West End restaurant where he had lunched well and expensively, Apple again got that feeling across his shoulders. He was intrigued.

The sensation came and went over the following hour, as Apple got on and off buses, boarded and alighted from Underground trains, got in and out of taxies. It was absent in the Marble Arch Odeon, where he fell asleep.

The sleep was unplanned. It happened when he closed his eyes to blot out the screen, where the hero was lighting a cigarette. Apple awoke to the crash of fade-out music.

Outside, he went back to his routine of being the hare for the hound. He used all the tricks he had learned in Training Six and had rarely had the opportunity of using. For another hour, he had a marvellous time playing spy.

When Apple got home to his apartment, the telephone started to ring. Tossing his package aside, he went to the instrument in the living room. He lifted the receiver to hear:

"Christ it's you, etc., etc. I've tried to get you three times today."

"I've been out and about."

"Listen," June said. "Did you 'fess up?"

Apple told about his call to Watkin. "A piece of cake with fancy icing."

"That's good. We were idiots to— Oh!" There came the sound of a thud.

"What?" Apple said. "Hello?" There was no answer, though the line was still alive. It buzzed. There were vague noises. "Hello? Are you there, June?" Still no answer.

Apple stood straight and tense. Foolishly, he shook the receiver. Putting it back to his face he shouted, "What the hell's going on?"

June said, "Hello. Sorry about that."

Apple let himself go into a sag of relief. "What happened?"

"Well, I'm in this pub. Came in from jogging. My shadow probably thinks I came in to go to the john. While you and I were talking, I saw a face I know flash on the television, so I went out to ask someone what the item was about. It was on the news."

"Yes? And? What face?"

"Joe Ross's. It seems he came down with some mysterious virus this afternoon. He has a high fever. He'll be in bed for at least a week."

"Oh."

"So you," June said, "will be running for Britain in Paris."

CHAPTER 4

The athletes' village lay out in a countrified suburb, five miles from the inner suburb where stood the stadium. Each of the sixteen participating nations had its own wedge-shaped plot. This, about an acre in size, held three prefabricated buildings: dining hall, men's hostel, women's hostel.

The points of the wedges, which had gates, met at the rim of an inner park. It covered five acres. Like the plots, it was dotted with pine trees and had a neatly shaven lawn. It also had flowering bushes, a miniature lake, and stretches of ornamental wall that served as seats.

The total area would have been pretty had it not been for the fences. These, of the chain-link type and topped with barbed wire, separated every wedge from its neighbours as well as circling the whole village. The fences were ten feet tall.

Security was sternly tight, movement restricted. Those athletes who were not away at the stadium could fraternise in the park between the morning hours of ten-thirty and twelve, the afternoon hours of three till five.

Each inner gate had one armed French guard, while the outer

had four. They scrutinised the identity badge, with photograph, which all were obliged to wear. Athletes could leave the village only with permission from the head coach, though greater freedom was allowed to officials and pressmen. The latter had previous clearance and wore the same identity badge as everyone else. There were seven representatives of British newspapers staying in the United Kingdom sector.

Security was tighter than expected because of a recent upsurge in the activities of a terrorist group. The New Free French, which was non-political, specialised in arson, bombings, and extortion. Police had heard whispers that the group planned to try for the headlines it loved by some form of violence during the international track-and-field meet, either at the village or at the stadium.

All these details Apple saw or learned during his early morning settling-in period at the hostel, after flying over from London with the whole UK team and then busing out to the village. He also learned that there would be two eight-man heats later that day for the three thousand metres, the first three in each being the six runners for the final on the last day.

Apple further learned, while heading with the others for the outer gate, to bus to the stadium for the parade, that Bill Burton was present. The stout man fell into unsteady step beside him and said, his eyes sleepy, "This is further notice. Hello, Apple."

"Hello, Bill." He peered down at the lapel badge. "Does the *Daily World* know about this?"

Burton smoothed his bowtie. "They were glad to oblige. Upstairs lets them have some of our best leaks."

"I have a feeling I saw another familiar face a minute ago. But I don't think he's playing press this time."

"Forty-one, you mean? No, he's doing security. On loan from Scotland Yard, it says on his papers."

"It all seems a bit much to me."

"Well, off the record, it's nothing to do with that stupid terrorist scare. It's old Angus. He's being extra careful because this is an operation on loan, as it were. He wants to shine for the Mayflowers."

Apple asked, "How many back-up men do I need?"

Bill Burton shrugged. He said, "By the way, thanks for taking me to the movies the other day. I enjoyed it, as well as needing the rest."

Apple would have answered except for seeing June. She was beyond the fence, boarding the women's bus. Burton veered off, saying a loud, "Thank you, Mr. Porter."

Apple hurried, but before he got through the gate the bus was drawing away. He nodded to himself. Forty-one being here was for the same reason Bill Burton had tailed him in London—after his call to Watkin about the dinner with June. She and he would be kept well apart. Any success in the operation mustn't be tainted with the idea of assistance from the CIA.

That was fine, Apple mused. But if Upstairs thought it could keep him away from June, Upstairs had another think coming. But he would have to play it crafty.

The following two hours was a bore of waiting, of parading around the stadium, of standing in the centre during the making of five speeches and the playing of sixteen national anthems. Apple was glad to get back in the bus with some of the others, leaving the field to shot putters, long jumpers, pole vaulters, and javelin throwers.

Back at the village, Apple went up to the small dormitory he was sharing with five other men. It was on the upper of the building's two stories. Like the others, Apple changed out of uniform into casual clothes—jeans and a sweater. He left the room and set off for lunch.

At the bottom of the stairs, agent Forty-one was standing. A wry expression covered his sallow face and a cigarette dangled from his lips. Smoke came out with his indifferent, "Hi."

Apple nodded and went to go by, but stopped as the man said, "Hold on a sec."

"Want me to invite you to lunch?" Apple asked, crafty, crafty. "So that you can protect my valuable person."

"You're the funniest man I ever met, Thirty-four. And my lunch can wait, as can yours. They'll keep it warm for you, I have no doubt."

Apple, his gums watering, eased back from the smoke. "I dare say that if I wait around long enough you'll tell me what you're talking about."

The agent said, "You need a quick sauna. Right now."

Apple thought about it.

He said, "I see." Turning, he went along a corridor. At its end he stripped naked, left his clothes on a bench, and picked up a towel from a pile. The nearby door led him into a mildly hot room.

In the next room, hotter, Apple saw through the steam a seated figure enveloped in a toweling robe with a cowl that came down to hide the face.

Modestly holding his towel in front of him, Apple went across and sat beside the figure. He knew he shouldn't have done that, should have waited to be approached; not because of service etiquette, but because it would be spoiling Angus Watkin's love of mystery and surprise. But Apple had no need for the time being of rubbing his chief the right way.

He said, "Good day, sir."

Watkin grunted. He stayed in the same forward-leaning position. Apple thought it a pity he couldn't see his chief's face and its possible expression of disappointment.

"First of all," Angus Watkin said, "the race this afternoon.

Your heat. You will come in third, thereby qualifying for the final."

"Third, sir? Just like that?"

"Just like that, Porter. The race is fixed."

Apple drew a hand down his face to clear it of sweat. So as not to treat Watkin to too much disappointment, he allowed his voice to express the surprise he was feeling as he asked, "It's all arranged for me to come in third, sir?"

"Precisely."

"Five of the seven will be given a slow-up drug, I imagine."

Angus Watkin sounded happier. "Of course not. This is an international affair. One or possibly two runners could be doped, with a great deal of trouble, but not five."

Apple pampered, "Then how has it been managed, sir?"

"Mainly by cooperation. Only the East German and the Polish runners couldn't be got at from above, for obvious reasons. They will be first and second. Sweden is playing its usual role of neutrality and would put no whisper in its athlete's ear. But he likes money, and has been paid a nice sum of it—half down, half later—to not give you any trouble."

Apple wondered if the Swede would ever see the second payment. He asked, "And the other four?"

"They are under instruction from their governments, who are cooperating on a share-of-information basis. No doubt they will battle among themselves for fourth place."

"But surely, sir, their governments can't force them to run a deliberately bad race."

Angus Watkin sighed. "Don't be naïve, Porter. I had begun to think you were improving, what with the guile and the lying. Don't start to slip back, please."

"No, sir," Apple said. He recalled what his athletics-history teacher at Damian House had said: many star athletes were given well-paid jobs, at which they worked only superficially, thus having ample time for training and the attendance of sporting events. Those jobs could be withdrawn.

Watkin said, "The Italian, French, German, and Spanish runners will give you no trouble. They may not like it, but that's neither here nor there. You have an easy heat ahead of you, Porter."

"Yes, sir. Thank you."

"If it weren't for the cooperation, of course, you would be left far behind, as you would have at Liverpool had it not been arranged otherwise. These people are world class."

Apple asked, "And the final, sir?"

"That's an entirely different matter," Angus Watkin said. "All you have to do there is put on a decent showing. You will lose, but that's all right."

"I see."

"You don't see at all, Porter. Or do you?"

"Well, no."

The hooded figure gave a small movement that seemed to signify satisfaction. After a pause, Watkin said, "Your contact, Igor, is in fact called Igor. Igor Kazov. Is it familiar to you?"

"Vaguely. I think he's a runner."

"He is. In the last Olympics he won two gold medals—in the three thousand metres and the five. Nowadays he concentrates only on the three. He's coming down from his peak, though he is still a formidable runner. In Russia, he's a folk hero, and has been for five years. He's twenty-four. Look at this."

From within the robe came a hand. It was holding a photograph. Protected by plastic from the steam, the picture showed a man with a wide, square-jawed face, a flat nose, and small eyes. The brow was shallow under close-cropped fair hair.

"Got it?"

"Yes, sir."

Watkin withdrew the picture. "He looks a moron but isn't.

Not that he's terribly bright, either, but bright enough to be very, very careful."

"He'd need to be, sir, if he's constantly coming through the Curtain."

"Well, there's a performance to go with the caution. Igor pretends to despise all capitalists. He refuses to mingle with them socially—Kazov will not, for example, put in an appearance in the central park here. Frequently he declines to shake hands with fellow athletes on the track. He acts it up generally, along with his genuine prima donna attitude, all to the delight of the Russians."

Apple said, "But surely, sir, the KGB must find it odd, Igor having so much money to use on his playboy activities."

"They assume that he brings home luxury items, which he sells on the black market. They don't mind that at all. They deal there themselves. And he does, naturally, take back a certain amount of goods, both for himself and to help the assumption."

"As you pointed out, sir: super-careful."

"Also," Angus Watkin said, "he receives a wage for his work, which is in the chemical industry. When at home, he puts in two or three afternoons a week at a Moscow government laboratory. And that, Porter, brings us to the matter of information."

A formula, Apple was thinking even as his chief went on, "It takes the shape of symbols and numbers. Formulae. This time it's connected with a process for making food out of seaweed— food fit for human consumption. The Russians are several miles ahead of us in this field."

Well at least, Apple thought in relief, it's nothing to do with germ warfare. But what would he do if it was? Back out of the operation? He didn't know, and let the matter die there, wiping it off as quickly as he now again wiped the sweat from his face. He would have given Angus Watkin a happy domestic life for the gift of one cigarette.

"What the process is, Porter, I don't know, just as I have no idea how the Americans get payment to Igor Kazov. He refuses to make any personal contact with anyone from the West except in the manner which he invented himself."

Risking the disapproval of his chief for being correct, Apple said, "He passes the info over verbally during races."

The cowled head turned toward him. Angus Watkin's bland face had only a slight film of perspiration. Apple thought, Even in his body, the man's not bloody human.

"Verbally, Porter, yes. But hardly *during* a race. There would not, surely, be the breath to spare for long converse."

"Quite so, sir."

"What Igor Kazov does is give the contact the information while the runners are on the track, warming up, waiting to be called to the line. He gives it in fits and starts while he's moving around. He's extremely good at this, as, naturally, he needs to be if he wants to save his skin. If the formula is lengthy, he gives the rest of it after the race is over, while the runners are recovering."

"It's neat," Apple said. "Full marks to Igor."

Angus Watkin turned away. "Yes. I doubt if I could have come up with a safer scheme myself."

Which, Apple thought, was the highest praise possible. He said, "Pity Igor wasn't in today's heat. We could have had it all over with on the first day."

"Some things simply cannot be wangled," Watkin said. "And why Kazov fell out with his last contact, by the by, is that the CIA agent made the mistake of beating him in a previous race they were both in."

Apple nodded. He also understood now why June was unable to be used as a contact for Igor. She was the wrong sex. Everything was fitting together.

"That, I believe, is all," Angus Watkin said, in dismissal. "Have a nice race, Porter."

The stadium was packed. The noise from the sixty thousand people formed a constant rumble, with thunderclap bursts erupting every time a notable moment occurred on the field below. There were rabid chauvinist sections, where flags waved and rattles tolled monotony.

Most calm were the ones who were creating the excitement: the athletes. Next came the officials, particularly the timekeepers. Last were the armed policemen who, ignoring the sporting events, stood at regular intervals along the wall to the stands and looked up at the spectators.

Apple was there. His identity badge hung on the chest of his track suit, under which he wore running gear. He was waiting for the imminent women's mile.

By the time Apple had showered and dressed after the sauna, he had found the dining hall empty; by the time he had finished the light, pre-run meal, June had left for the track. Apple had left soon after, in a mini-bus with four other athletes, a patrol car behind and two police motorcylists ahead.

The loudspeakers began to blare. From the giant mouth of the entrance came a file of women. The leader and the one who brought up the rear were uniformed officials. The eight in between wore singlets and shorts. The former bore national initials on the front, a number on the back.

June's deceptive UK was performing a gentle hula to the music of her breasts. She was stern-faced. Marching with swinging arms, she looked to be full of confidence.

Apple dithered and twitched nervously throughout the wait, while the girls limbered up, did stand-still running with knees high, charged back along the track in short bursts of running.

He was coated with sweat when they were finally called to the start.

The pistol was fired. It sent the eight leaping forward, from which charge they seemed to slow as they settled into a pattern against the inner lane. June was lying fourth.

The leaders drew ahead slowly until there were two separate groups of four. June was in front of the rear pack. After the second lap, she was overtaken by one girl, then another, then the last. The three stayed together. They soon left June behind.

Apple watched sadly, even though knowing that this was inevitable. He watched the race being won while June was only just entering the final lap. He watched her, misty-eyed with pride, as she kept up her furious pace while knowing the cause was hopeless. He watched her.

The starter raised his pistol. Apple, in the premier position by the inner line, was prepared for the crack. When it came, he went forward into a steady, lasting run.

The others hurried past to make up the valuable yardage. They jostled for positions. They had not settled into a single line until the first quarter-lap had been covered.

Apple kept his pace the same. He felt relaxed, fine, fit. It didn't bother him that the others were stringing out and drawing ahead. The race was fixed.

Not until after four turns of the oval did Apple begin to put on the force, though without exerting himself too greatly. He was still running in comfort.

Slowly he drew level with the man in front. He was Italian, his singlet initials informed. Apple said, "Hello."

In Italian the man said, "It took you long enough to get here, you long-legged bastard." He blinked with shock when Apple answered fluently in the same language, saying, "I know, but I've got a stone in my shoe."

The man recovered. He asked imploringly, "Mind if I stay close behind you?"

"No. But not too close. And don't blame me for all this. I've got orders too. Come on."

Apple moved ahead. He was sorry for the Italian, whom he could hear pounding behind, but he reminded himself firmly that all was fair in love and spying.

Soon he was drawing level with the next man. From the march-in he knew him to be from West Germany. Passing, he said in German, "Nice day for a spin in the country." He told himself that this was ridiculous, feeling that he had to speak to each of the forced losers.

The man shot him a vicious glance. With a strong Bavarian accent he said, "Go spin your head in a cement-mixer."

"It's all in a good cause, old man."

"It better be. Go on, piss off."

Apple moved on. He was having to work hard now. The competitors were so good that their second best was equal to his first. It took him longer to catch up to the next runner, who had long blond hair streaming out behind him.

The Swede asked in English as Apple came alongside, "Would it be okay if I got the second payment in dollars?"

In flawless Swedish, Apple said, "Maybe. If you go a bit slower."

"I thought you were British."

"I am. But I've been taking lessons. For weeks. Slow down."

The Swede asked, "And I'll get US dollars?"

"If you don't slow down you'll get nothing," Apple said, and then found himself pulling ahead without any extra effort on his own part. From behind came the pounding of three sets of shoes.

The next man was close, yet it took half a lap for Apple to reach him. He was breathing with difficulty now. It was no easy task for him to speak. In Parisian French he gasped, "Sorry about this. Not my fault. You can win another time." Apple wondered worriedly if he was going to blow the whole caper by dropping back out of sympathy.

The Frenchman said, "Be no other time for me."

"What d'you mean?"

"It's my last race. I've had this business. It stinks to hell. I'm retiring."

"No," Apple panted. "Don't retire. This won't happen again."

"For me it won't," the Frenchman said. "Get moving."

Apple drew ahead and asked himself how many years these people had spent training, perhaps especially for this one occasion. He groaned. It was no help that he was passing a section of British sports fanatics, who screamed their encouragement at him.

Chased by four sets of drumming feet, Apple ran on. The East German and the Pole were close together, well ahead. Between was the last of the fixed runners, a Spaniard. He kept glancing back. The next time he did so, Apple sent him a sympathetic smile.

When he finally came abreast of the dark-haired man, he was shattered to see that there were tears in his eyes. Apple panted, "*Lo siento mucho.*"

"You're a countryman of mine!" the man said, also in Spanish. "How can you do this to me?"

"It's all in the name of peace."

"Think of my pride. I could take this race."

"I can't help it. Don't blame me. Please."

"Everyone's watching on television back home," the Spaniard said lugubriously. "My wife. My children. My parents."

Oh God, Apple thought. I can't do it. He said, "Don't."

"Listen. Tell you what. Get behind me and step on my heel. Let me lose with grace."

"Yes," Apple gasped. "Good. I'll do that."

"I'll pull ahead," the Spaniard said. "Good-bye and ten thousand thanks." With ease he ran on, while Apple veered in toward the inside line. He thought with hope/horror that the arranged accident might cause him to fall himself.

He was right behind the Spaniard but couldn't get close enough. He shouted, "Slow down!"

The dark-haired man looked back. "What?"

Apple felt a jolt in the toe of his right shoe. Next, all was confusion. He saw a whirl of crowd and sky and grass. He heard a cry of alarm come both from himself and the Spaniard. He felt a jolt of meeting bodies.

Then Apple was in the centre of the asphalt track, stumbling semi-sideways, wheeling his arms to keep his balance. He saw the Spaniard lurch into the Frenchman, who staggered against the Swede, who tottered into the German, who fell over onto the Italian. The five became a tangle of broken runners.

Apple recovered, stopped careening. He turned fully the other way and ran on. The Pole was crossing the finish line one stride ahead of the East German. It was another ten seconds before Apple reached the same place.

After crossing, he slowed to a long lope. Slowing still more, to a walk, he looked back. The Italian was leading the other four across the line.

Apple continued at a walk along the track, hands supporting his back. He felt relieved and not too physically distressed. Absently he listened to the loudspeakers booming name and time of the winner, name and time of the man in second place . . .

After that, silence.

No longer absentminded, Apple came to a stop. He turned. The runners were bunched together, talking to a group of officials. As Apple watched, the loudspeaker system came back to life. It said that an objection had been raised by the Italian team manager.

Apple went cold in the core of his burning body. If the objection was allowed, he would be out of the final. But he saw with hope that the Italian runner was vehemently shaking his head. The German, Swede, Spaniard, and Frenchman began to shake theirs.

Apple started to walk back. He kept his fingers crossed.

"You were lucky," the discus thrower said gloomily. He was a huge Scot with a red beard like rusty steel shavings. In his event, he had placed second. "Very bloody lucky."

"Yes, I could've got tangled up with the rest of 'em."

"I don't mean that. I mean getting away with treading on the wee laddie's heel."

"It was an accident," Apple said indifferently, craning his head to pinpoint June, who was over at the other side of the dining hall.

The Scot put a fist-size piece of meat in his mouth and chewed rapidly. Swallowing, he said, "Aye, it was. Certainly. It's an accident if I get my toe out of the ring when nobody's watching." He added, as Apple got up, "You don't have to leave."

"I'm not," Apple said. A fast glance around showed him that Bill Burton was talking at one table, while at another agent Forty-one had his eyes on his plate. Apple stared at June.

She had already seen him. She nodded when he gave a slight jerk of his head to mean that they should meet outside after dinner. Apple sat again and went cheerfully back to his food.

Leaving the last topic, the gloomy Scot talked about how poorly the British team had done so far at the meet. "Except for me, of course. And there's sure to be a first from Mary Brand in the high jump. She broke the world record last month."

"Good for her."

Threateningly, the discus thrower said, "Her mother was born in Glasgow."

In a minute, June and several other athletes of both sexes rose in a group. They began to drift out. June knew better than to look back.

Apple hurried through the rest of the main course, deciding against dessert. He had been late at the dining hall. On returning from the stadium, he had been forced by coach Percival Reed to have a rest, which Apple had insisted he didn't need, but during which he had fallen asleep.

"And there's Staple in the marathon," the Scot was saying. "He might pull it off."

"I'm sure he will," Apple said, rising. "His father's from the Highlands."

"Is that a fact?"

Apple moved away from the table. He was seen both by Bill Burton and Forty-one, who at once began preparations to leave. Apple went on and outside. Like June and most of the others, he wore jeans and a sweater.

It was a mild, bright evening, with dusk still an hour away. Apple strolled between the chatting groups, the couples and the moody loners. He went toward where half a dozen athletes were sitting on the grass with June.

She, Apple mused, could have been ordered to tone down the touch-me-not attitude. Or perhaps the others were showing their sympathy for her dreary performance in the mile.

As Apple joined the group, sitting on its rim, he noted that Forty-one had come out of the dining hall. He was leaning against a tree, drawing deeply on a cigarette. Apple looked away. He knew that so long as he and June weren't by themselves, there could be no cause for complaint.

When a lull came in the talk, he smiled at June and said, "Good try, Miss Greystone-Cairn."

"Thanks awfully. But do call me Marcia. Congratulations on getting in the final."

The other athletes murmured variations on the same sentence. By their dead-eyed manner, Apple guessed them to have already competed in their events, and failed. So this gathering could be neither orders to June nor sympathy from the others, but a case of losers sticking together. Apple realised he was still a novice in the world of sports.

When the shots sounded, all talk in the wedge-shaped sector ended. People looked at one another, groups exchanged glances. June raised her eyebrows at Apple, but he didn't know what it meant either.

The burst of firing had come from the far side of the central park. In the following silence, just when people were beginning to shrug, another round of shots sounded.

This one was louder. Which meant it was closer. It had come from somewhere over to the right, beyond the Netherlands section next door.

June brought her eyebrows down into a frown. Slowly, Apple began to get to his feet. Someone in the group suggested nervously, "Could it be fireworks?"

Before Apple had reached his full height, there came a third burst of gunfire. It was so loud, so close, that it made Apple jerk rigidly erect, while the other sitters leapt to their feet with exclamations of shock.

Apple swung around to face the direction of the noise. It had come from the area of the perimeter fence, which was out of sight behind trees and the women's hostel.

As Apple hesitated, with cries of alarm all around, he saw agent Forty-one running toward the fence. He also heard more shots from the first two places. He ran after the sallow-faced agent.

Passing Bill Burton, who was sitting on the grass, Apple came in view of the high link fence. His legs stuttered him to a halt. He instinctively drew back. He stared.

The action was outside the gate. There, the policemen were standing with their arms stretched high in the air. Covering them were seven or eight men. They had sub-machine guns of an old-fashioned design and the strangest appearance Apple had ever seen.

The men were in white from tip to toe. They wore boots, ski suits and tight gloves in white. Their hair was hidden under white rubber bathing caps. A white paint or cosmetic covered their faces and necks.

Even while gaping in apprehension at the terrorists—for this had to be the New Free French—Apple was admiring the disguise technique. The ski suits changed body shapes, the caps made the heads like a million others, the facial features were obliterated by being rendered void of shadows.

Apple wondered if all this could be a joke of some kind. But then he noticed the blood-spattered policeman lying some yards farther back, beside an overturned motorcycle.

Apple's total observation had lasted mere seconds. It was so brief that the action seemed to have been frozen. Now the picture moved. Four of the terrorists in white came striding through the gate.

There were a dozen or so people left within view of the attackers—others having run back toward the buildings. They sent their arms rigidly aloft when the tallest terrorist barked in French, "Hands up! Nobody move!" Without the words, the gun gesture was sufficiently eloquent.

Apple, farther away than the rest, took one long, fast step to the side. It brought him into the lee of a tree trunk. He peered cautiously around its edge.

One of the people with raised arms was agent Forty-one. He was putting on a good act of being a terrified civilian.

Near him the four men in white stopped, though spread in a line. The tall leader asked, "Where's Mary Brand?"

Forty-one shook his head. In English he said quaveringly, "I don't understand you. I don't speak French."

Which was a lie, Apple knew. If Forty-one didn't understand French he wouldn't be on this operation. Apple also knew now what the attack meant. Here and at two other sectors, the terrorists intended taking a hostage, who would be one of the stars with an international name.

As he began to back carefully away, keeping the trunk between himself and the men in white, Apple mused that the kidnap victim would either be used for ransom or to extort the release of terrorist colleagues at present in prison. No hostage would be a French national. That wouldn't put the government in an embarrassing enough position.

To his secret pleasure, feeling like a pro, Apple further mused that it could be extremely awkward if one of the hostages turned out to be Igor Kazov. Then he felt embarrassed for not considering the danger to Mary Brand.

The leader was repeating his question elsewhere. He shouted it viciously. A man answered in badly accented French, "I think she is near the gate to the park."

Apple continued walking in reverse. From around the trunk he saw one of the terrorists, who then saw him. Apple turned and ran. The man shouted, but Apple had already dodged around another tree. Then he circled another.

He ran on, threading between trunks. A glance back showed him that three of the men in white were coming at a trot, leaving one behind to guard the people near the gate.

Apple came in sight of a scattered group—athletes, officials, kitchen staff. Everyone stood in a crouch of worry. His eyes picking out the high jumper, Mary Brand, Apple shouted to her, "Run! Run away and hide!"

The advice was taken as general. With one exception, everybody began to run. People crashed into each other. Some fell down. They were tripped over by others. Girls screamed.

Mary Brand ran to a nearby tree and threw herself upwards. She caught a branch, hauled herself up and was quickly lost from view among the foliage.

The exception to the escape attempt was June. She stood calmly, warily still. Her eyes were on Apple, who was approaching her fast. The mêlée was clearing by the time he was almost there.

"Terrorists," he called to her. "Get out of sight."

June moved quickly into action. She ran toward a tree as Apple veered aside to the trunk of another fir. He stood behind it. He gasped: June, trying to emulate Mary Brand, leapt for a branch and missed.

She fell, sprawling on her back. Apple, about to rush from his hiding place to help, held back because of the three things that happened next. They happened simultaneously.

The terrorists arrived in the area, where now June was the only one left; Bill Burton, smiling, weaved into view opposite Apple; police car sirens began wailing in the distance.

The men in white came to a stop. They were looking around in sharp, jerky movements. Sweat glistened on the white faces. The three were slightly forward of where Apple stood, obliquely between him and Bill Burton, who now ended his amble and said, "Hello, boys. Is it time for the circus?"

While one man pointed his machine gun at him, the leader aimed his weapon at June. He snapped in French, "Tell me where the Brand girl is. Quick!"

June moved up into a sit. She stretched her arms out at the sides in a gesture of helplessness. "I don't understand you," she said in English.

Bill Burton called over to her, "No parley vooley Frenchy?"

The leader snarled at Burton, "Silence, you drunken idiot." He took a step toward June. In English of a kind he said menacingly, "You no tell, I kill."

The other men glanced behind them as the police sirens grew louder, then gave anxious-seeming attention to their leader. He thrust the gun out, saying, "I kill. Now."

Giving a samurai scream, Apple burst from behind the tree. At the edge of his vision he could see the three men reacting with startled spasms. He ran toward June. As he was throwing himself in front of her, three shots rang out in rapid succession.

I'm dead, Apple thought. He hit the ground with a jolt. But he had no pain, except winces from the fall. He shook his head and whipped a look back.

The three men were drooping. The leader had dropped his gun, the others were letting theirs sag toward the grass. The pure whiteness of the terrorists had been sullied. Roughly in the middle of each man's forehead was a small, round red hole.

Apple looked aside. Bill Burton, his face grave and alert, was in the act of putting a revolver back in a waist holster that his jacket would normally hide.

He said in a bored voice, "There goes my cover."

Depleted, Apple said, "Fantastic aim."

"It wasn't bad."

"You're not drunk, of course."

Burton shook his head. "Never took a drink in my life."

The terrorists continued drooping, fell to the ground and lay still. Apple felt a tinge of nausea. He was glad of the diversion when the police sirens reached their post-finish crescendo, which was followed by a chatter of gunfire from the direction of the gate. The next diversion was even better.

Apple was fallen on by June. She mumbled a thank-you. They embraced and rolled over, a tangle of arms and legs. Their mouths finding each other, they began to kiss. It was fervent, excited kissing. They held to the embrace tightly.

Soon, Apple was aware of voices. The people had come creeping back now that there was silence everywhere. They seemed to be sharing their curiosity between the necking couple and the three white bodies, though they appeared to prefer the quick to the dead.

Realising that he was lying on top of June, Apple rolled over, but without breaking off a kiss. Now he was underneath, and he thought this almost as unseemly as before. He brought June alongside him on the grass.

"What's going on here?" asked an indignant voice. It belonged to Percival Reed.

Faces first and bodies next, Apple and June eased apart. They looked up. Foremost among the surrounding spectators was the fat coach, his arms assaultingly folded.

Apple had nothing to say. June, however, immediately took to her cover. Freeing herself from the remains of the embrace, she leapt up. She raised both hands to her face and stood with shoulders hunched, as if she were acutely embarrassed.

"Good heavens," she said as Marcia Greystone-Cairn. "How awful of me. How frightful. How quite, quite frightful. I must be in shock."

She went on in the same vein, accepting pats of comfort from other girls, as Apple got to his feet to face from a high point the agitated coach.

"Most improper," Percival Reed said. "To mention nothing of the damage to your nerves. You must rest at once. Come with me. I'll get the doctor to give you a sedative."

Managing to look sheepish and nerve-shot, Apple followed the coach through the crowd.

When Apple awoke from his sedated sleep, it was still evening, twilight making the room dim. He sat up and yawned. He nodded yes, he was feeling fine, to the question from an athlete who was sitting on one of the other beds.

The man was the Scots discus thrower. From him Apple learned about the attack.

The raid to capture hostages had failed entirely. Only in the British sector had terrorists actually penetrated a compound. At the Danish and West German gates they had met resistance. In all, there were eleven victims of the affair: seven terrorists, one security guard, and three French policemen. The track meet was to continue regardless.

"Only an earthquake could stop it," the bearded Scot said. "This is sports, after all."

"Yes, indeed."

"They'll have a two-minute silence in the stadium tomorrow to honour the fallen."

Apple got up and lifted the towel from the foot of his bed. Nodding, he left the room. He cut himself off midway through wondering if the dead terrorists had wives and children. Don't go back, Watkin had said.

Apple met Bill Burton at the washroom door. The scar-faced agent looked spruce but glum. His bowtie sagged at the edges and there was no identity badge on his lapel. He said a dull "Hello."

Apple touched his arm. "I know, Bill. It can't be an easy thing, killing people, whoever they might be."

Burton shrugged. "That doesn't bother me. I've totalled before. It's only the first time that's bad."

"So what's up?"

"I'm leaving. My cover's gone and I'm being pulled out. In fact, Upstairs might even retire me."

"For what happened today? But that's ridiculous. You probably saved somebody's life."

"That's got nothing to do with it," Bill Burton said. "I had no right to interfere. I stayed away from the action at the gate, as did the Yank girl, who's a real pro, but then I had to go and stick my nose in."

"And quite properly."

"No, Apple. On an operation, you cling to that operation. Nothing else matters." He put out his hand. "So long."

They shook hands firmly. Apple said, "Good-bye and thank you. One of the lives you probably saved could've been mine."

Burton winked and moved on.

By the time Apple had washed, he felt better about Bill Burton and his predicament. The service pensions were generous. Apple felt altogether fine, fresh, keyed up, and in the mood to be out and about. He felt like seeing June.

Leaving his towel in the small dormitory, where the Scot was snoring, Apple went to the stairs. He was halfway down before he saw a security man sitting on a chair below. Apple stopped.

Smiling, he asked, "What time is it, please?"

Expressionless, the man checked his watch. "A little before ten. Bedtime for all good athletes."

Apple went back to his room. Crossing to the aluminium-frame window, he looked out into the gathering dusk. People were moving around among the trees or sitting on the grass, though no one was too close to the building. It was a tranquil scene, with no suggestion of the violence and death of scant hours ago.

Apple shortened his gaze. The drop to the grass he guessed to be about four yards. High, but not all that high for a man of six feet seven inches.

The sash-type frame slid up easily and silently to Apple's lift. Bending, he leaned out for a second appraisal of the area. He sighed as into view strolled agent Forty-one, who was looking up at the window.

"Nice evening," Apple said.

"Yes, it is. Good night."

Apple laughed. "Don't tell me you thought I was about to sneak out like a kid."

"I'm not telling you a damn thing, Thirty-four."

Although Apple didn't like the man, he was forced to admire him for his cool action earlier by the gate. He said, "Listen. If I give you a note will you see that it gets to you-know-who? That wouldn't be breaking any rules. You can even read it. And I'll put in a good word for you with old Angus."

Looking pensive, Forty-one got out a packet of cigarettes. He lit up, with Apple gazing away to his left. After his second drag of smoke the agent gave a perfunctory nod.

"Okay, give me your note. I'll see that it gets there."

"Hold on." Apple went back in, found paper and pencil, scribbled two lines asking June to meet him in the park at eleven the following morning, folded the paper and returned to the window. Throwing the note out, he said, "Thanks. When this caper's over, I'll buy you a pint."

"Make it two," the agent said, stooping to pick up the paper. He straightened. "Good night."

Apple closed the window. He went to lie on his bed, but he was too pent up to rest. He was feeling the after-effect of the day's excitement, a delayed reaction. Also, his nap had taken a large bite off his need for sleep.

Apple knew, however, that no matter how long he waited, even until long after midnight, the exits would be watched. It wasn't worth the chance. He would have to wait for the morning.

Apple got up and started to pace.

He saw the night draw on, watched his other dorm mates come in and retire, prowled the silent corridor. It was in the early hours before he felt tired enough to lie down, and it was an hour after that before he finally fell asleep.

Apple awoke to sunshine. Still muzzy, he automatically reached for the bottle on his bedside table. He shook free one blue pill, got out of bed and sloped across to his locker. After adding the pill to the collection in his bag, he realised that the other beds were empty. His watch showed ten o'clock. He hustled along to the washroom.

The dining hall was deserted, except for staff. They made no complaints about serving a late breakfast. Apple ate quickly. All his life he had made a point of being early for appointments, in case the other person were also early and felt slighted if Apple merely managed to be prompt. And in this case, the person was something special.

It lacked several minutes to half past ten when Apple headed for the gate at the thin end of the wedge. Other athletes were bunched together there, waiting for the guard to open the padlock. Joining on behind, Apple turned, thinking he might see June. Instead, he saw Forty-one.

Apple sighed. He went to meet the agent and asked, "Are you going to follow me around in the park?"

"Only more or less. So long as you stay with a group, there'll be no problem. Sorry."

"Okay. Did you deliver my note?"

"I gave it to the women's coach at the dolly hostel. She'd see that it got to Miss Mayflower."

"Thanks." He went back to the others, who were filing through the newly opened gate.

In the park, Apple strolled. He didn't look behind. He waited for five minutes, until he had set an aimless, guileless pattern; waited until he was rounding a large flowering bush. Then he moved swiftly.

He ran to the bush's other side, saw that Forty-one still hadn't come into view, leapt across an open patch of ground to a second bush, and from there hurried to a third.

No one gave him away by staring; sudden bursts of running were the norm here rather than a rarity. The way he now peered in a crouch around the bush might have caused curiosity, but not enough to draw the attention of his shadow.

Who came into sight at a fast pace and went out again behind the first mass of flowers. Apple took off like a hundred-metres man. He headed back the way he had come. Glances behind showed him that all was clear.

Apple didn't slow until, between trees, he could see the gate, through which people were still strolling. With these, as had happened with Apple, the guard gave no more than a cursory examination to identity badges: the danger was over and unlikely to be repeated.

Stopping under a pine, Apple did a Mary Brand. With his height he needed only a light leap to grasp a branch. He pulled himself up and then step-laddered his way up the tree. When he was sufficiently hidden from the ground, but had a good sighting on the gate area, he stopped and used a branch as a seat. He hummed a tune.

His humming ended as his lips formed involuntarily into a smile. Now he felt more convinced than ever that in June he had found a true soulmate. She too believed in being early. It was only twenty minutes to eleven, yet here she was, coming through the gate.

June didn't look around searchingly. She didn't hesitate. She didn't dally over which direction to take. There was purpose in her manner as she strode off toward the left. Her features were set in a serious cast, though she flicked on a smile in answer to the greeting of an athlete she passed. After that, her dimples disappeared again.

Apple stopped considering whether he should drop down casually or swing to the ground with a Tarzan yell. He thought that obviously June must have decided on a particular spot for their meeting; that it was somewhere they had mentioned, or one that she had concluded he had meant by her interpretation of his note.

Apple began to climb down. The only possibility that occurred to him was that June would be going to the lake, which lay in the exact centre of the park.

When he reached the ground, June was well ahead. He followed at a casual pace. Between keeping a sharp lookout for Forty-one, he watched the rhythmic sway of June's hips in the snug jeans.

June answered more greetings while she walked. Apple also got his share of passing attention, which, he noted, had an element of deference. Not only was he a finalist, he had been involved in the climax of yesterday's fracas.

June stopped to talk to an athlete. Apple dawdled off-course, straightening again when June moved on. A minute later he did the same thing when June stopped a second time, but he himself came to a halt on seeing that in June's attitude there was an essence of finality.

The man she was talking to wore T-shirt and shorts. Of average build, he had a ruddy complexion and fair hair. He looked to be in his mid-twenties. He made a healthy, clean-cut figure as he stood with feet spread and arms folded.

Apple moved to the side of a tree and went on watching. He blinked slowly. His spirits sagged. He could see that what was going on ahead was more than a friendly chat between new acquaintances.

June stood in a forward lean, as if listening with care. She had her hands clasped behind. Although her face was visible only in profile, the expression it showed seemed to denote something close to devotion, which matched every other aspect of her manner.

Apple's mouth sagged open. His whole being throbbed with the ache of jealousy.

He told himself he was an idiot. He was jumping to the wildest conclusions. June's attitude meant nothing. It was due either to misconstruction on his own part, or a standard facet of the Marcia Greystone-Cairn persona. She might not even know the man.

So what was she doing here? sneered Apple's Iago.

There could be many reasons, Apple answered. She might be delivering a message for one of the other girls—there *had* been gossip about romances budding to life between the various nationalities. She could have seen Forty-one and had stopped to talk to this man, a stranger, in order to mislead the agent or to warn his quarry.

Iago asked, Is that the way a girl, any girl, would look when she's talking to a stranger?

All right, he's known to her but only by name. They've never met before. He's a world-famous athlete and she, with her life-long interest in sport, is responding to him the way your average girl would to a favourite movie star.

That's neat, Iago said. Good invention there. Fast, too. So he's a big name, eh, and she just happened to know exactly where in the park he'd be at eighteen minutes to eleven?

This time Apple was slower. At last he came up with, It's a business matter. Of course it is. The man is her Control, a new one because the other couldn't swing this kind of cover.

Iago: Have you ever heard of a Control younger than thirty-five?

June and the athlete both glanced at their surroundings. Apple snapped alert. He looked around for cover—at which point he realised that he already had it.

He was standing behind a bush and peering through its leaves. Without realising it he had moved into hiding during the time he had been watching the pair ahead.

And that time, he saw, checking his watch, was less than a minute, though it had seemed like half an hour. June couldn't have done more than give the stranger greetings, or pass over the message of that other girl, or begin to express her admiration for the sports-world star, or exchange the signals of Control and operative.

June and the man started to walk on, side by side. Carefully, Apple followed. While moving from one patch of cover to another, he assured himself that he was not jealous. Jealousy was juvenile. It was a sign of insecurity. Insecure he was not. He had the strength and self-confidence of a rock.

Apple twitched on seeing June's arm touched by the man in shorts, whose other hand was pointing. The pair moved aside to four low lengths of ornamental wall that were formed in a cross. They sat on one of the arms, facing this way.

Apple backed off. Loping, he began on a wide circle. He arrived well to the rear of the walls and from there started on a cautious approach. He thought he would probably ramble up and say, "Ah, there you are." Except that it wasn't eleven o'clock yet.

He came to the last item of cover, a tree. Between it and the walls lay an open space twenty feet across. He wanted to get closer, but if June or the man glanced around . . .

Apple chanced it. He strode briskly to the nearest wall-arm, where he shot down to an all-fours position that took him out of sight. He asked himself what he was doing.

If he intended eavesdropping, he ought to be ashamed of himself. It was disgusting, despicable, outrageous, and totally out of character. Iago told him not to be naïve. He had every right to know what was going on. He was involved with the girl, wasn't he?

And, Apple told himself, brightening, she might be in some kind of trouble. That was why she was here with this sinister-looking character. She could be the victim of blackmail. Anything.

Apple noticed that he was being observed. From some distance away, a girl was staring at him with interest. He uprooted a daisy and brought it close to his face, though continuing to watch the girl from the corners of his eyes. She walked on.

Apple sank prone. He lay the side of his head on his folded arms. When he was sure he had no other observers, he began to shuffle along beside the wall.

Despicable, he thought.

Soon Apple could hear the voices of the pair. He shuffled on. The language they were speaking was German. Although content was blurred as yet, Apple could hear enough to know that the man was native to the tongue and that June had spoken the truth about her command of the language: her accent was perfect, her construction poor.

Apple stopped his shuffling when the voices became reasonably clear. He improved on that by raising his head until it was almost level with the top of the wall. He listened.

"I can understand, yes," the man was saying, "that there are certain difficulties in this case. But nothing so severe that it can't be overcome."

June said, "I don't know if you do understand, not fully."

"Please remember that I am not without experience myself. You obviously know that."

"Yes, of course."

A famous runner, Apple told himself. June had come to ask his advice about running the mile.

The man said, "You have had every opportunity and you have been given all the help you needed."

"I know, I know," June murmured, and now Apple realised from the tone of her voice that what he had earlier taken for a devoted manner was, in fact, subservience. He listened in growing uneasiness as the man continued to complain and June to murmur defensively.

"I believe we chose the wrong person for this job," the man said at length. "That's what it boils down to."

"It was hardly a matter of choice, if you don't mind me saying so. I was the only one who could do it."

"Yes, there is that. Still, I'm not satisfied, and neither is anyone else. More is expected. You must get closer. No more delay. Is that clear?"

"Yes, it is," June said. "I'll try my best, comrade."

Apple lowered his head in the following semi-silence: there was the sound of body movement. He closed his eyes and listened to June and the man walk away. He felt as empty and dead as a used cartridge.

So, Apple thought after a moment, June was working for the other side. That was her reason for being here, possibly her reason for showing a romantic interest in string-bean Appleton Porter—the one to whom she had been ordered to get closer. But it could be some other matter altogether that she was working on.

Whichever, whatever, June was a Sickle.

Tiredly, Apple sat up. He didn't even make the effort to be

cautious. Not that it mattered, for there were no signs of June and the man. They would have gone their separate ways, and June would now be planning to keep her eleven o'clock date.

Apple got up quickly. He set off running, heading for the gate to the British wedge. If he were to meet June now, in his present state of distress, he knew he would be sure to give the game away.

Apple reached the gate safely, passed through and ran on to the male hostel. He went inside and upstairs. To his relief, he found the dormitory deserted. Throwing himself on the bed, he thought about it, his decision.

Was he or was he not going to tell Angus Watkin?

The decision, Apple realised, was actually something else. What was more important to him, the operation or the girl?

He tried to answer that with yet another question: Was he in love with June? But he didn't know, and therefore wondered about the times that he had "known," been sure that he was in love. He counted on his fingers while remembering, which mental exercise gave ease to his troubled mind.

Apple stopped counting at twenty-seven. He told himself that the large number didn't mean that he wasn't really in love this time. But then again, it would be part of June's training to be able to make a man fall for her, the way a con artist's stock-in-trade was to beguile his victims.

Apple tried to think badly of June. That didn't work. He could only see her as the person he knew, not an enemy. Still, he persevered in this to the extent of considering the how of her placement.

June was either an American Communist, Apple mused, or a well-trained Sickle who had been planted in the States years ago. She had slowly worked her way into the CIA. Or she could have been converted to the Moscow line once established as an agent. Or she was a stand-in, the real June having been kidnapped somewhere in transit between Maryland and London.

Apple liked the last best. He thought that possibly even June's Yank-tourist Control was part of the scheme, a Hammer; and that British Intelligence had been completely taken in. It was, after all, a fairly short-term operation.

But did Upstairs suspect? Was that why he and June had been kept apart, beyond what seemed reasonable?

Apple got up and started to pace. Avoiding decisions, he mused that June's aim in the operation must be to find out how certain pieces of information were getting through the Curtain. The Reds would have tied the leaks time-wise to international sporting events. Which, because of his own induction, meant that the suspects had been narrowed down to the three-thousand-metres man Igor Kazov.

The affair was growing more complicated by the minute. Apple, finding the room confining, went out and began to pace the corridor. He strode swiftly.

In retrospect, he could see the flaws that he had previously accepted without question. June had poked around off her allowed route at Damian House; he had seen that himself. And hadn't it been a bit too convenient, her being out in the field behind the pub in Little Wentworth? Walking with him there, she had fed him bits of information about Liverpool: standard procedure in gathering is first to give. She had been the one to make contact in London, by telephone, thereby opening the way to a date.

Apple paced on, his nerves begging for a cigarette, until men began to come in, to wash before lunch. Apple went back to his bed. When the Scots discus thrower entered the dormitory, Apple said he wanted to conserve his energy.

"So would you bring me back something to eat, please?"

Although the last thing he felt like right now was food, Apple knew that an empty stomach would be no help. But he didn't want to go to the dining hall and see June.

It was later, while forcing down a steak sandwich, that it occurred to Apple that June could be tripling, not doubling. She could be a genuine agent of the CIA, who had planted her on the KGB, who thought they had wormed her into the Central Intelligence Agency. All this could be unknown to British Intelligence. The present coziness of the two secret services was, after all, a little peculiar.

Apple swallowed and put his sandwich aside. He grew so excited by the new idea that he had to go back to pacing in the corridor. In any case, the Scot and another man were snoring through post-lunch naps.

Making a turn at the top of the stairs, Apple met the up-directed gaze of agent Forty-one, who said, "When're you going to eat? I'm starving."

"Not hungry. I had a big breakfast."

"And then did a neat job of shaking me in the park."

Apple shook his head. "Unintentional. And I didn't even speak to the Mayflower. She was being chatted up by some guy. Danish, I think. So I came back here."

"I saw that," Forty-one said. "When I lost you, I watched her. And he's not a Dane. He's from East Berlin. A dud. Came last in the five-thousand-metres heat. Sure you wouldn't like a snack?"

Shaking his head, Apple moved away. He continued his pacing. The news in respect of nationality and race-placing cooled his excitement. The facts removed the possibility of him having made a mistake.

Also, Apple thought, wasn't he too stridently looking for a loophole? At the same time, he was trying to make June into the reverse of what she must be, turn her from a sordid two-face into a storybook, super-spook, glamorous tripler.

Even so, Apple clung to the idea with one mental fingertip as he continued to pace.

It was another hour before he reached a decision, which he abrogated within five minutes; another two hours before he again decided, changing his mind within thirty seconds; another three-quarters of an hour before he came to an irreversible conclusion. In his whole life he had never spent such a miserable day.

"You've got to do what?" agent Forty-one asked.

"Talk to Watkin. It's urgent. So how do I call in?"

"You don't. This isn't London."

"That fact has managed to penetrate my brain," Apple said coldly, gazing down at the operative. They were standing in the lower hallway of the hostel. "I'm quite bright at times."

Forty-one flicked on a lighter and put flame to the cigarette in his mouth. He drew in smoke luxuriously, exhaling along with, "Contact here is for an emergency. Of the dire variety. You ought to know that."

"I do. And this is dire." An awful truth, Apple told himself, for had his decision gone the other way he would feel no better. He was playing traitor whichever way he faced. He was probably an idiot for putting duty before self, but there was no going back.

"You'd better tell me what's up, Thirty-four."

Apple took a step back from the smoke and stared off into the distance. "I talk to no one except my chief. Either you tell me how I make contact, or I report you for falling down on the job. You are, I assume, my back-up man."

The agent took his cigarette away to speak, but Apple went on, "I repeat that this is an emergency. I don't want to have to say it a third time. I know more about this caper than you, as you may possibly have guessed from our numbers. So let's get on the ball, or you might find yourself called Three-hundred-and-one. Forever."

Although Apple ended on a curt nod, at the same time he was fighting an urge to give the man an apologetic smile.

Forty-one, his sallow face twitching, said, "Okay, okay, don't lose your freckles. I'll tell you how. But it's on your head, not mine. And the emergency better be so dire it floats."

"Let me worry about that."

The agent pointed. "The doctor's room's opposite the sauna. Go and tell him you have a severe headache over the left ear."

Apple's hesitation was short. The oddity of the instruction fitted the pattern of what was normal in the field. He turned away without another word and strode along the passage to the last door. He knocked, was called on to enter, went into a poky room.

The doctor was young and keen. Through large spectacles he looked hopefully at the visitor. Hope turned to a disappointment tinged with worry when Apple said he had a pain. "Right here."

Fifteen minutes later Apple was sitting in the back of an ambulance. With its siren off, it was being led at a normal pace by one motorcycle policeman. The intern, in grubby whites, lay on the stretcher and told sleepily of his hectic job.

They stopped on a busy street in Paris. The British security man who had ridden in the front took Apple into a building and up in a lift. They went through a door which bore the name of a medical specialist, passed through an empty waiting room, entered a passage. The only sound was that of a child singing a television commercial.

The security man (straight, Apple judged) halted at a door. "The doctor's expecting you, Mr. Porter."

Apple went into the room. It was a den, with two easy chairs, in one of which sat Angus Watkin. He said, "You're too late for tea, I'm afraid. Please sit down." His tone indicated that he found this visit tedious. "You have a problem?"

"Yes, sir," Apple said, sitting in a slump. "We all have. In respect of Miss Mayflower."

"I hope, Porter, that you're not going to tell me that you have developed a deathless love for the young lady."

"No, sir. I've been keeping my distance. Or at any rate, as much as I could in such a confined area. But yes, this morning I did get close. And—enter the problem."

Watkin, head back, hands clasped in his lap, was watching him steadily. "Go on."

"I saw her talking to an athlete from East Berlin. Curious, I crept up close to hear what they were talking about. I confess to playing spy. It's not often I get the opportunity."

"Point taken, Porter. But to the gist."

Apple told about what he had heard. Angus Watkin displayed no emotion. He asked, "How's your total recall?"

"Not of the finest, sir. And in this case I wasn't prepared for absorbing. But I can try to give you the exchange as verbatim as I can."

"Do that, please."

When Apple had finished, Angus Watkin moved his hands to the chair arms and drummed his fingers lightly. It seemed like the action of a man who was contented, though the face gave nothing away.

Trying to be equally bland, hoping not to show his anxiety, Apple asked, "Does it mean what we think it means, sir?"

"Oh yes," Watkin said airily.

"She couldn't be tripling?"

"No, Porter. The Americans aren't so foolish as to have kept a fact like that to themselves."

"Would it be foolish, sir?"

"Very. The young lady might come to harm otherwise."

Apple felt a familiar chill. It passed quickly when he got a thought that made him feel even worse. As a rapport was known to exist between himself and June, what if Watkin ordered him to cultivate her still more?

Apple said, "I wonder if I could have a meal out somewhere, sir, on the way back from here. I rate low on acting ability, as you know, and if I ran into the girl in the dining hall I might give the game away that we've tumbled."

"That can be arranged, yes," Angus Watkin said. "Don't worry, you won't be called on to play up phoney to the young lady."

Bloody mindreader, Apple thought, and then he winced as Watkin added a squelch: "This is a job for a top professional."

Doing a Watkin, pretending he hadn't heard, Apple asked, "Could this be a stand-in caper, sir? Could the real CIA girl be held prisoner somewhere?"

"Leave it, Porter. You've reported the incident, and that's as far as you go."

"Very good, sir."

Angus Watkin returned his hands to their clasp. He said, "Since you're here, I might as well give you your signal for Igor Kazov. Save me making contact tomorrow. All right?"

"Certainly, sir," Apple said, pretending interest.

"In the line-up, in the stadium entrance, before the runners are led out to the track, you will have a casual word with some of the others, and to Igor you will say, in Russian, *May the best man win*. He already knows about you, but this is for his own peace of mind. He is, as I've pointed out before, super-careful."

"Yes, sir."

"That is all, I believe, Porter," Angus Watkin said sleepily. "And do try to put on a decent show tomorrow. A few eyebrows have already been raised about the poor performance of Miss Marcia Greystone-Cairn in the mile. Igor Kazov wouldn't like it if you did something similar."

"I'll try my best, sir."

"Good afternoon, Porter."

Later, back in his room, after hamburgers and milkshake in an American-style drugstore, Apple found a note on his bedside table. It was from June. She asked why he hadn't turned up for the eleven o'clock date that morning.

Apple's try at a cynical smile merely produced a grimace. He put the note in his bag. He wasn't sure if this was because he wanted a memento of June, or if he thought that a sample of her handwriting might sometime be found necessary. It was the latter he opted for. He told himself, wretchedly, that he would be a pro yet.

CHAPTER 5

Next morning, Apple awoke with a feeling of urgency. He needed to be on the move. He wanted to be out and about, but he knew that his activities would be severely curtailed if he was to be successful in avoiding a meeting with June. He would, in dreary fact, have to stay in the hostel until it was time to leave for the race, which was at four o'clock. Apple couldn't stand the thought of such a lengthy imprisonment.

He made himself stay in bed while the other men were rising, dressing, and drifting off for breakfast. Lying on in the diagonal position that he always had to use in normal-size beds, he feigned sleep and planned how he would get out of the compound so that he could go into town.

Although Apple knew that he would probably be given permission to leave by the head coach, Percival Reed, that was too easy. He wanted to keep his mind busy. Furthermore, if he left openly, he would have the company of a shadow. Which formed problem number one.

When the last man had gone, Apple got up and put on shorts. From his bag he got a handful of blue pills. He went out, along the passage, and down the stairs, where Forty-one looked around from reading a paperback and said, "Good. I'm hungry."

"I have to shower first," Apple said. "Meanwhile, here's a present for you. In thanks for delivering my note yesterday." He eased the pills into the waiting palm.

"What are they?"

"High-strength pep pills. They give you energy, but they also make you feel very randy. Unfortunately. Because that's not what I need right now."

The agent smiled. "Well now, Thirty-four. I won't say no. Thanks a lot."

"My very great pleasure," Apple said, turning away.

Back in his room he collected his pale green uniform slacks and took them along to the washroom. He filled a basin with water, into which he put the trousers. When they were sodden, he brought them out and squeezed them to dampness. He put them on after stretching out the creases. His shorts gave him protection, but his legs felt clammy. The slacks, however, were now a dark green.

In his room Apple put on shoes and shirt. Next he donned a tweed jacket belonging to the huge Scot. Its shoulders hung down to his biceps, but that gave length to the sleeves, making them almost reach the wrists. To the lapel Apple pinned his badge of identification.

He went along to the room that was being used by the reporters. It smelt of gin. Two of the men were still asleep. Apple looked in the wastepaper baskets, hoping to find the press plaque that Bill Burton had worn and apparently discarded. The baskets had been emptied.

Apple went to one of the lockers. A plaque and badge were on a shirt. He quickly unfastened the one he wanted, and pinned it in place as he went out and along the corridor.

The hall below was empty. Refusing to think sympathetically

of agent Forty-one, who was probably throwing up in the lavatory, Apple slipped outside. The compound was near deserted, most people still at breakfast. Apple strode to the exterior gate.

It now had only two policemen. The glance they gave Apple and his lapel credentials was casual. He passed through and walked off in the direction of the city.

Half an hour later, following a ride on a bus, Apple was strolling along a wide, beautiful boulevard, his identification pocketed. There were trees, birds, and sunshine.

Here I am in Paris, he mused. So what?

The diversion of escape and arrival over, his trousers dried back to pale green, Apple began to think about June. So he was glad, presently, not bored or annoyed, when he got the sensation between his shoulders.

Apple cut off the boulevard. He came back to it after circling narrow streets for ten minutes. His back told him that he still had the shadow. The strength of the sensation told him additionally that his tail was not an expert at the job. That ruled out one of his own people or someone from the other side, unless, for some reason, the tail wanted his presence to be known to the quarry. Apple found it intriguing.

On a corner he stopped and looked back. He didn't try to pick out individuals among the many strollers. He simply took a mental picture of the various patches of colour.

Apple repeated this six times as he walked, crossing to the other side and again taking to the back streets for a while. He was finally left with an impression of red with dashes of white.

He stopped at a sidewalk cafe, where the tables were topped with umbrellas. Sitting, he looked idly along the way he had come. The girl was approaching. Her red dress was short, with white lace on the sleeves, hem, and low neckline.

Apple noticed that he wasn't alone in his watching. Others at the tables were appraising the girl—men with hunger, women in pique. What they saw was a voluptuous, long-legged creature with large breasts. She had shoulder-length hair of a rich auburn, and was probably in her low twenties. She was strikingly pretty.

Sure he had made a mistake, Apple expected the girl to go straight on past. But she moved over to the cafe, came to a table right next to his own, and sat with a sensuous movement that was like a grind minus the bump. At no time had she looked at him directly.

A waiter came. After taking Apple's order for coffee, he turned to the girl and got her order of a sweet martini. Leaving, the waiter started back as the girl produced a pack of cigarettes from her white purse. He fumbled for a lighter. At the same time, a man at the table behind was opening a box of matches.

Ignoring them both, the girl leaned toward Apple. She asked, "You 'ave ze flame, pliz?"

In French, Apple said, "Sorry. In any case, smoking is bad for one's health."

The girl sprang on a look of delighted surprise, which, Apple decided, was genuine. She said, "Ah, but your French is perfect. You cannot be English, and yet you look it so terribly much." While talking, she put the cigarettes back in her purse.

Apple smiled, nodded, looked away. He wasn't about to give any assistance. But what, came the thought, if the girl had followed him and was making a play simply because she found him attractive?

The thought was so outrageous that Apple felt the beginnings of a blush. The better to picture the blowtorch, he closed his eyes. On opening them again, he saw that the girl was sitting down at his table.

"I will confess to you at once," she said, "that I have been following you for some time." She smiled, showing unusually long eye-teeth, which Apple found erotic.

He asked a pointless, "Really?"

"And now, as you can see, I am forcing myself into your company. But perhaps you are accustomed to this kind of thing, mm?"

"One can get used to anything after a while." This was equally pointless but sounded clever.

The girl pouted sexily. "I suppose you think I'm mad."

"You don't look mad."

"Thank you."

"You look extremely sane," Apple said, glad to be not thinking about June but wishing he had the protection of a cigarette, or a matchstick.

"Then you must think I'm cheap."

"You don't look that either."

"Ah, I have it now," the girl said. She nodded shrewdly. "You have come to the conclusion that I'm a harlot."

"I have come to no conclusions whatever, mademoiselle."

"My friends call me Coco. It's silly but I like it. Now you must tell me your name."

"It's Peter."

"And you actually are British? I can hardly believe it, your French is so good."

"I'm English and I'm a tourist."

"Only a tourist?" the girl said, putting on another pout. "I'm sure that isn't true, Peter. I think you must be something marvellous and mysterious."

"No. I'm simply seeing the sights of Paris. Sorry to let you down. Tourists are awful."

The girl waved both hands like a double good-bye. "But no. I won't hear of it. Tourists are fascinating. They put on a new skin when they go abroad. They enthrall me."

She leaned back in her chair, smiling at him, as the waiter served their orders. He did it untidily, his eyes mainly on the girl's cleavage. When he had backed reluctantly away, Coco said, "You look at my drink, I see. Therefore you have now decided that my behaviour is due to drunkenness."

Apple put two sugars in his coffee. Stirring, he said, "I do not, necessarily, think that you're mad, cheap, a prostitute, or an alcoholic. But what are you, Coco?"

"I am a free-lance graphic artist. I don't do terribly well at it, but my father is rich so it hardly matters."

Apple liked that. Whether true or a cover line, it was good. But cover was difficult to accept, he thought. She wasn't the type. She was even more unlikely as an operative than himself.

Coco said, "You will, I'm sure, be wanting to know the reason why I have been following you."

"I will."

She leaned forward again. "The reason, Peter, is because I am fascinated by tall men. They do something to me which is hard to explain. My last boy friend was nearly two metres tall. You, I would guess, are taller than that."

"Slightly, yes," Apple said. He was musing that it could be. Could be she was telling the truth. Curiously enough, for the past several weeks, since the start of the operation, his height had been proving a boon rather than its usual drawback.

Coco said, "When I saw you a little while ago in the street, I said to myself that I had to get to know you. I could not help myself. I had to follow." She frowned abruptly. "Are you married?"

"No. But it wouldn't matter if I was. I'm a tourist and wearing a new skin."

The girl showed her eye-teeth again. She said, "Fortunately, I'm not shy. Otherwise we might never have met. And to make everything better, simpler, you speak my language. My English is poor, is that not so?"

Apple said, "Yes."

It was no fazer. Coco showed no response. Raising her glass, she said, "To your health."

"And to yours, which appears to be blooming."

"In the body, yes. I sometimes worry, however, about the way I am fatally fascinated by tall, tall men. Though I can't say it's ever done me any harm. Quite, in fact, the reverse." Her smile took on a different angle.

"How pleasant for you."

"And now, Peter, you must tell me all about yourself."

Apple sipped his coffee. He said, "Ladies first. You tell me the story of your life."

Thirty minutes later, pausing in pouring scorn on her Swiss finishing school, Coco looked into her empty glass and said, "But we must have another drink. Shall we order sweet martinis?"

Apple hesitated. He asked himself how he was feeling. He answered that he was amused and diverted and soothed in the ego. He said, "Why not?"

Thirty minutes after that, while Apple was finishing his second martini, Coco said, "Now it's your turn, Peter. You know all about me, I want to know all about you."

"Fair enough."

"But we would be far more comfortable if we went to my studio. Shall we do that?"

"Why not?"

It was not on the Left Bank, Apple was disappointed to discover. Nor did it have a large, many-paned, sloping window that afforded a view of rooftops and chimneypots. In no way at all was it part of the romantic tradition. Apple soon lost his disappointment, however, simply because he was feeling the effect of his two drinks on an empty stomach.

The studio was in a high-rise, which they reached by taxi.

The walls of the main room were painted red with white trim. Mess and a drawing board filled a smaller room. All windows looked out at other windows.

Coco pulled on white cords to snap closed the red venetian blinds. Pointing to a sideboard, she said, "Help yourself, Peter. I have to change my shoes. My feet are killing me but I insist on wearing high heels because I want to look taller." She went swayingly from the room.

Fine, Apple thought. So she's a height freak. Nothing wrong with that. In fact, it's probably the world's most sensible fetish. Obviously a highly intelligent girl. And one with the common sense not to allow herself to be frustrated.

Humming, Apple went over to the sideboard. From a bowl of fruit he helped himself to a banana. The skin he put on top of the sherry bottle after he had poured out a drink. He nodded sagely at the knowledge that there were hours and hours to go until the race this afternoon.

Coco called, "Go on talking. I can hear you."

Chewing and sipping, Apple returned to the story he had been giving in the taxi, about being a teacher of French in a London school of languages.

He said, "The only problem is the low ceilings. I keep on bumping my head."

"What are the girl students like?"

Apple swallowed the last piece of banana. Before he could answer, there came a sound like an audience hissing. It was pierced by Coco's call of, "What did you say?"

"I didn't say anything."

"I can't hear you, Peter. Come here."

After emptying his glass, Apple went out of the room and along a passage. The bathroom door was wide open. In the shower stall, facing the other way, stood Coco. She was naked. Water jetted down onto the crown of her head.

Clasping his hands behind comfortably, Apple looked at the sopping auburn hair that lay against the creamy shoulders; the trickles of water that chased down to the small waist; the shine on the outsweeping buttocks; the long and shapely legs. Coco was a magnificent animal.

She looked over her shoulder and asked, "Well?"

Apple said, "The girl students are quite nice."

"Oh. Good. Would you soap my back, please?"

Smiling muzzily, Apple went to move forward. He stopped when Coco said, "You had better take your clothes off, Peter, or they'll get soaked."

Apple slipped out of the tweed jacket. To take off his shoes he sat on the bidet, but got up again at once because he thought the position improper. He heeled the shoes off, then removed the rest of his clothes. Even though he felt not the faintest tingle of a blush, he was glad that Coco was turned the other way.

He went to the step of the stall. Splashes of water tickled him as he took the soap from its dish. He produced a lather between his palms and began to coat it across the smooth shoulders. He said, after clearing his throat, "Some of them speak French much worse than you speak English."

"Mmm," Coco murmured, swaying her hips. "That's nice."

"The beginners, of course, don't speak any French at all."

"I see."

"But they soon pick it up."

"Enough," Coco said, turning her whole body around with an abrupt movement. She smiled. "I mean, enough of that method of soaping."

"Yes," Apple mumbled. "Quite so." He didn't know what he was talking about.

Coco said, "This method is better." She took the soap from him and, moving forward, started to stroke it over his chest. "I will be very gentle."

"Thank you," Apple said huskily.

After putting the soap back in its dish, Coco, her face as full of concentration as an artist's, began to bring the coating to a lather with both hands. She worked with smooth dexterity, though her touch was light and sensual. She lingered on the thighs and the stomach.

Straightening, she said, "Evidently that was to your liking, Peter."

"Yes," he said tightly.

"Now we can do a proper soaping." She stepped back under the shower to wet herself, returned and swung around, and started to rub her back against him with slow and sinuous twists. Apple whimpered.

Coco turned. Without losing flesh contact she moved around until they were face to face. With Apple's chin resting on the top of her head, she repeated the gentle rubbing. Her breasts squirmed on his ribs like carried water bags. Her thighs slithered repeatedly past his own. He was unable to whimper.

Moving back, Coco took Apple by the hand and drew him into the shower. They stroked each other until there was none of the bubbly lather left.

Coco switched the jets off. Crooking a finger at Apple, she led the way out of the stall. They dribbled water out of the bathroom and into a bedroom, where Coco broke the silence with, "Ah, my hair is a mess."

"Doesn't matter," Apple gasped.

But Coco had already changed direction, moved her aim from the bed to a vanity table. There she grabbed up a brush, made two ineffectual strokes at her tangled hair, opened a drawer and closed it again with the brush inside it. She turned.

"You're right," she said. "It doesn't matter."

They went to the bed.

A quarter hour later, lying entangled among damp sheets, Coco and Apple looked at each other and said, "Hello."

Coco had a gleeful, satisfied expression in her eyes. That was how Apple's body felt. He hoped his eyes didn't show that he was feeling a double traitor toward June—because, he insisted to himself, that was not the way he was feeling at all. He was feeling absolutely first rate. Fine. Super. Great.

Coco sat up. She said, "Health hazard or no, I'm going to have a smoke. How about you?"

Apple said, "Why not?"

It tasted divine. It tasted like woodsmoke floating over a field on a summer evening. It made his throat tingle with love and gratitude.

Apple had two more cigarettes before Coco snuggled back into his arms and whispered, "This time, we don't need a shower."

After the second bout, Apple fell asleep. Slowly coming to the surface of consciousness, he found himself alone. He yawned and stretched. From the kitchen came the sound of singing.

Apple remembered the vanity table. He got off the bed and went to the drawer, which he drew out quietly. Beside the hairbrush was a framed photograph, which, as there was nothing else in the drawer but jars and tubes, must have been the object that Coco had wanted to get out of sight.

Apple turned the picture around to look at the face. He nodded. Although neither the man's name nor nationality came to him, he recognised him as one of the finalists in the three thousand metres.

Closing the drawer again, Apple looked sadly at his reflection in the mirror. He told himself he might have known.

However, in moving back to the bed Apple also moved away from the personal. He mused in defence of athletics that the runner might not be a party to this scheme to weaken a rival. Coco could be doing it herself, out of love. It was a pity it was a waste of time, after all her sacrifice and planning: the British entrant offered no threat to anyone in the race.

Presently Coco entered the bedroom. She was wearing a tight, short T-shirt, and nothing else, which made Apple clench his toes. He pulled the sheet over himself and reached for a cigarette.

Among the tangled bedding Coco put down a plate of delicate sandwiches and an earthenware jug. Mugs of the same clay hung from hooks on the jug's rim.

"We'll feast before we continue the festivities," Coco said. "The sandwiches are smoked salmon, and this wine is an excellent year."

So excellent that the label can't be shown? wondered Apple. Or decanted in order to be doctored? In fine, was the wily young wench trying for more than a weakening—a complete absence from the race?

Apple said, "I hope you're going to drink with me."

"Oh yes. Of course."

Which, he mused, meant nothing. She might be looking forward to a sleep herself after her labours.

Apple stubbed his cigarette and looked at his watch. He had no need to act surprised. It was one o'clock. He said, "You'll have to drink it all by yourself, I'm afraid. I have to go."

"Go? But you can't leave before the feast."

He crammed two of the sandwiches in his mouth as he got up. He went on keeping his mouth filled as he fetched his clothes, followed by Coco, and while he hurriedly dressed. This served to ease his hunger and simultaneously made it impossible for him to answer Coco's repeated question of why he had to leave. He merely rolled his eyes at her. At the apartment door he gave her a crumby kiss before slipping out.

On the street, Apple lost his acted haste. There was time and enough for him to get back to the village, to rest before being driven to the stadium.

After asking a passer-by for directions, Apple began to walk. The sun was high and strong. It hurt Apple's eyes. That, after a while, made his head start to ache. The bolted sandwiches seemed to have stuck midway down; they sat in a hard lump of indigestion. The alcohol inside him was turning sour. His throat felt raw from the cigarettes. Certain muscles complained from the activity in which he hadn't indulged for some time.

Apple soon felt, all in all, quite rotten.

He hailed a cab.

At the village, Apple took off his tweed jacket after passing through the gate. The compound was deserted. Almost everyone, he guessed, would be at the stadium for the various finals, either participating or watching.

When Apple walked into the hostel, agent Forty-one looked up from where he was sitting on the bottom step of the staircase. His face, normally sallow, was now a whitish yellow.

He asked feebly, "Where the hell've you been all morning?"

"Hiding in a tree. I don't feel well."

"*You* don't feel well? Listen, I've been puking for hours."

Thinking that he might do the same any minute now, Apple brushed by and began to trudge up the stairs. "Must be something you ate."

"I haven't eaten a bloody thing all day," Forty-one said. "I've seen the doc and he says it must be a bug. Maybe you ought to see him as well."

Apple made his climb crisper, which hurt. "I'm okay. I'll lie down for a while." He reached the stairhead and went along to the mini-dormitory, which was deserted. He took his identification off the discus thrower's jacket before putting it away.

On his bedside table lay a folded piece of paper. He opened it out. From June, the note asked a simple, "Where are you?" Dropping it aside he let himself sink tenderly onto the bed.

Minutes later, he was beginning to drift into a doze when Forty-one came in. He was accompanied by the doctor, who blinked his hope and asked, "It's not that pain again, is it?"

Apple shook his head on the pillow. "I'm fine," he said without conviction or interest.

The doctor used his stethoscope, felt a pulse, lifted an eyelid. "No discomfort anywhere?"

"None," Apple lied.

"No vomiting?"

"No."

The doctor straightened. Dully, he said, "It must be something like stagefright. Pre-race nerves. A condition along those lines."

"Then I'll recover," Apple said, closing his eyes again. He heard the man leave. Next he knew, he was being shaken awake. He said, "Yes, I'm ready to go."

"It's not time yet," agent Forty-one said. "You're wanted on the telephone downstairs."

"I don't want to talk to anyone."

"Yes, you do. Up you get."

Apple dozily allowed himself to be hauled up to a sit and from there to his feet. He was more alert by the time Forty-one ushered him into a room below and closed him in alone. He went to the desk and from it lifted the telephone receiver. "Hello."

"Well, at least you're alive," Angus Watkin said.

Becoming even more alert, Apple said, "Yes, sir." He patted himself on the chest, as though he could be seen by his chief. "Alive and well."

"There seems to be some doubt as to that—the wellness."

Although he felt better than before, it was still a lie when he said, "I'm fine."

"The doctor and Forty-one are mistaken?" Angus Watkin asked. "They are possibly lying? Perhaps deluded? They have been looking at the wrong person? They have decided to play an elaborate practical joke on me?"

"I think they've made a mistake, sir. It's Forty-one who's been sick today, not I."

Angus Watkin said heavily, "I am not, Porter, referring to a physical condition."

"Oh," Apple said. "Oh?"

"The problem would appear to be psychological."

"Yes, sir."

"But we know, you and I, that you are not suffering from first-night nerves, because there is nothing to be nervous about. We also know that you are not worried about danger, because the operation is danger-free as far as our end of it is concerned. And we know that you are not afraid of having trouble in memorising the information that will be passed on to you, because you've been tested recently in that area and not found wanting. Am I correct?"

"Well, yes you are, sir."

"Good, Porter. Excellent. Then you know, of course, the exact nature of the problem."

Apple shook his head before saying, "I'm afraid I'm not quite following you, sir."

Watkin's sigh was long, which meant he was happy with himself. He said, "You are suffering a despondency, Porter, if not an outright depression. This could very well tend to make you produce a poor performance in the forthcoming race. Which would look strange. No one would be happy about it."

"Obviously, sir."

"It should be equally obvious to you why you're despondent.

153

It no doubt is, for you aren't a dullard. Only shy. A trifle diffident. You probably find it difficult to admit the truth."

"The truth, sir?" Apple asked, puzzled as well as unsure if he was being flattered or insulted.

There was another long sigh before, "You have had two notes from the young American lady, Porter. That, possibly, has kept alive what I referred to as a deathless love and which you denied. Let's call it an infatuation, shall we?"

Apple began to understand, see the misconception. He said, "If you wish, sir, yes."

"Thank you. Most kind. And because of said infatuation you are now in a state of despondency. That, Porter, is the truth which I would like you to admit."

In a tone that he hoped would indicate reluctance and defeat, Apple said, "Well, all right. Yes. I suppose that that's what it boils down to."

"Splendid. Good man. Therefore all we need to do to get you in good running form is cure you of your despondent mood. Which cure can be easily brought about."

Apple stood straighter. Looking all around the room, he took a better grip on the telephone. Carefully he asked, "Are you going to tell me, sir, that the young lady is, after all, tripling?"

"No, Porter, I am not."

"Oh."

"I am going to tell you that she is not even doubling."

Several seconds passed before Apple began, "Not even . . ."

Angus Watkin said, "What you must understand, Porter, is that your devotion to duty was in question. There was a previous failing to be considered."

Confused, Apple asked, "A failing? You mean the meeting at Little Wentworth?"

"No, I do not. Nor the *accidental* meeting in Leicester Square. But that's beside the point. There was a failing. You needed to be tested. Therefore, Porter, a test was arranged." He paused. "You see?"

His mouth open, Apple nodded. See he did. Clearly. All his confusion was gone. He understood exactly what had happened.

Word of his note to June about the eleven o'clock date in the park had been given to Watkin. He had arranged a set-up with June and a supposed athlete, one whom agent Forty-one later identified casually as being from East Berlin. They had talked in German in a way that made it plain they were on an anti-West operation.

And I fell for it like a lamb, Apple thought. Then spent a terrible day agonizing over the decision of whether or not to report the doubler.

Even while his fury at Watkin grew, Apple was seeing how well done the set-up had been, even to Forty-one acting reluctant to tell him the way to make contact with his chief.

Angus Watkin asked, "Still cogitating, Porter?"

"No, sir," Apple said coolly. "It's noon clear. But—" He didn't finish. He had been about to ask why Watkin hadn't told him as soon as he had reported June that it was all phoney. But he knew the answer already. It was a typical double-handed Watkin deal. In a way that no order could, the set-up had kept Appleton Porter from further contact with the CIA operative.

"But what, Porter?"

Hit suddenly by another realisation, Apple blurted, "But this means that June is straight." His fury evaporated. He blinked, smiling.

Angus Watkin performed his third long sigh of the telephone conversation. "That is what I just told you, is it not?"

"Yes, sir," Apple said briskly. "It certainly is." He felt like shouting. He almost felt an affection for Watkin. "You have explained the matter most concisely, sir."

His chief said a dry, drawled, "Thank you."

"Not at all. Entirely welcome."

"I gather from your tone, Porter, that your despondency has been dispelled. Good. Now perhaps you will be able to put on a decent, unsuspicious showing in the race."

"I will, sir, yes. You may depend on me."

Following a short silence, which, Apple knew, was intended to signify cynical doubt, Angus Watkin terminated the call with a light, "Good afternoon, Porter."

Apple dropped the receiver into its cradle from on high. He brought his hands together and milled a happy circle. Striding to the door, he yanked it open and went outside.

Agent Forty-one was waiting. His face was less lemon-coloured. He asked, "Did you have a medical before you were given those pills?"

"Yes," Apple said. He meant it as an apology.

"That's the answer then. They don't suit my particular system."

"It might interest you to know that some three percent of women are unable to take the Pill."

"It doesn't, not at the moment," Forty-one said. He nodded toward the room. "You've had your problem solved as well, I can see."

"Yes. And I can understand why old Angus used the girl in his loyalty-to-duty test."

"Sure. After you pulled that big hero bit when the terrorists were here, she was the obvious choice."

Which isn't what Apple had meant, but it fitted, and it also fitted that Angus Watkin wouldn't have told Forty-one about the secondary reason.

The agent looked at his watch. He said, "You'd better start getting yourself organised."

Apple ran to the stairs and up.

It wasn't until he was being driven to the stadium that his euphoria paused. The smile which had been in place constantly since Watkin's telephone call drooped at the corners. The sharpness went out of his body.

Apple was realising that, of course, June had been a party to the set-up in the park. She had been one of the principal actors in the neat playlet. She had contrived against him.

Putting on the defence counsel wig, Apple offered that June had been under orders, obviously; an operative did only what he or she was told to do. She hadn't liked it, but she had been forced to obey.

In the prosecutor's wig, Apple asked why, in any case, had she not told him of the phoney spy scene as soon as she knew that he had reported it. She could have sent a note to that effect, or asked to see him.

The wigs went back and forth. A note might have been sent, but confiscated. That wasn't likely. She might not know he had already reported the playlet. That was even less likely. She might have been told he had failed to report. So why had she sent the two notes?

The trial went on.

Apple stayed in his hiatus, neither happy nor unhappy. There was a piece of further evidence that teased his memory. The prosecutor fought to bring it forward from the back of his mind, defence counsel managed to keep it there by taking a keen interest in the road, the walk from parking lot to stadium, the descent to a labyrinth, the talk of others in the United Kingdom dressing room.

When Apple was changed into running gear, sitting waiting, the head coach came in. Percival Reed's fat face was flushed with excitement. Sitting on the bench beside Apple, he began to give a pep talk. Apple didn't listen, not after latching onto the word *fail*.

That was the mnemonic the prosecutor wanted. It brought forward Angus Watkin's mention of a "previous failing."

Discarding both wigs, Apple thought about it. If the failing was neither the visit to Little Wentworth nor the dinner date in London, then it had to be the muggers—that is, the fact that he had not reported the incident. And only one person had he told of Green-suit and Coveralls. That person was June. She must have passed on the word to Upstairs through her Control.

Apple sagged. He sat on, staring dully at the animated face of Percival Reed, hearing nothing, while absorbing this new and dreary information. He felt hurt. It was a different emotion from when he had believed June to be working for the other side. That was disappointment. Now he felt personally abused, and used. He felt like going to sleep.

Noticing that the head coach was standing, Apple rose also. Percival Reed said excitedly, "So, Mr. Porter, we will give our all, won't we?"

"Yes. I suppose we will."

"Off we go."

Apple was shaken by the hand and wished luck by the other men before leaving the room. He followed the fat coach along a passage and up flights of stairs. They came out into the brightness of the high entrance arch.

As though his charge were a child, Percival Reed shooed Apple over to where were gathered officials and the five other finalists for the three-thousand-metres race.

Apple picked out Igor Kazov at once, recognising him from the photograph he had been shown in the sauna by Watkin. The Russian was average in height. His face was simian, with a flat nose, small eyes, and a low forehead. His fair hair, cut short, was ruffling in the light breeze.

Igor Kazov stood apart from the others. He stood with back straight and arms folded and chin high. He looked to be posing for an artist who was creating one of those Red murals wherein the hero appears ready to give his life for his tractor.

Thinking without too much interest that Igor was overdoing it, Apple went to one of the athletes and offered his hand. After the perfunctory shake, he strolled over to Kazov. In Russian he said, "May the best man win." Igor gave a curt bow-nod. Apple moved on to another of the runners.

In a minute, the chief official began arranging the athletes in their allotted places, the same positions that they would take up on the starting line. The crowd was booming, the loudspeakers were giving out the result of the previous event.

Apple felt that he was being stared at. He looked around. The starer, he saw, was Percival Reed; and the horror in Reed's eyes, he realised, was because he, Apple, was working his way through a long, long yawn. He turned away indifferently.

The line of six men was formed. Apple had a good place: third from the front. He couldn't have cared less. Glancing behind, he saw that Igor Kazov had the penultimate position.

The loudspeakers crackled, whined, began to announce in French the next race. They were repeating in English when the chief official, at the head of the line, raised his arm. He swept it forward like a wagon-train guide. The men moved off.

On the track, not bothering to emulate the smart march of the man ahead of him, Apple searched the stands. He knew where most of the United Kingdom athletic contingent would be gathered—close to the section of rabid British fans, with their flags and rattles.

Apple soon picked out June. This was because she wanted to be easily pinpointed. In reverse of the standard one-of-the-herd procedure, she was wearing a headscarf and a sweater of the most eye-attracting colour, bright orange. She was one row back from the front.

That June looked particularly pretty increased Apple's hurt.

He wondered how she dared. He tried to keep his attention else-where as the line of marchers drew closer, but was unable to stop himself having another look.

Their eyes met. June, standing, mouthed elaborately, *"What is wrong with you?"*

Apple turned his gaze down. He was relieved/wretched when now, short of the British section, the marchers were brought to a halt. Think operation, he told himself.

Breaking out of line, the athletes began to limber up. Apple knew better than to make any sort of approach to Igor Kazov. That he would leave to the Russian. He walked up the track, turned his back on the British section and began to do knee bends.

One man went sprinting by. The next to approach was Igor. He came slowly, taking long, taut, muscle-stretching strides. When still some yards from Apple, he began to speak. His lips barely moved. He gave numbers and letters.

Staring down at the asphalt, Apple concentrated. When the voice ended, Igor Kazov having gone by, he repeated the se-quence to himself, then did so again. He was about to start on another repeat when the voice came back: Igor was making his return.

Apple mentally recorded the second sequence with greater ease. He was accustomed now to the situation and the coarse voice. After doing a final knee bend, he moved to a different point on the track, where he started to sprint in one spot.

Igor Kazov, standing near another athlete, was wheeling his arms. He kept this up for so long that Apple wondered if all the information had been passed over. Then the Russian began to come across, head down, arms still wheeling.

When close he hissed, "Three more sequences."

Apple huffed through his half-open mouth, "Be quick." He kept up the sprinting while the voice lasted, though changing his pace so that every footfall matched a syllable. That seemed to pound it into place in his head.

Igor went on past, leaving two more sequences to go.

Apple stopped sprinting. He began to walk in a circle. This he stopped as the starter called, "To your marks!"

The six men stood in the same pose: left leg bent, right leg straight and with its foot toeing the white line, arms poised for action, head forward and down.

Apple could sense the tension of the other men because he had none of it himself. He was going to do his best but he wasn't wound up to the bursting point. What occurred to him as the starter raised his gun-holding arm was that he would never be able to tell her how much orange suited her.

The starting-pistol cracked.

As one, the men rushed forward. The noise of the crowd swooped up from its steady rumble to a blare, as if everyone had been hit by a splinter from the non-existent bullet.

After some seconds of confusion and bustle, the runners formed themselves into a single file. Apple saw that he was in third position, the same as at the start. Ahead of him, a yard and a half away, was Igor Kazov, lying a sensible second.

There was no change after half a lap.

The British section came into view. Apple couldn't stop his eyes from going to June. As he moved closer, as her features became clear between the splashes of orange, he could see that she wore a frown of puzzlement.

From behind Apple came the pounding of footfalls. They grew steadily in volume. Their owner, a man with a beard, came level. He was passing Apple as they drew near to where June was standing.

Apple slowed minimally so as to let the man go past, thereby giving himself a clear scan to June. Locking eyes with her he mouthed, *"You told about the muggers."*

Apple switched his attention back to face the front. He told himself that he was being childish. Next time around, he would ignore her totally. He had to concentrate on the race; on being sure of coming a respectable last.

The bearded man was cutting in toward the inside line. He made it even though Apple picked up on his pace, putting it back to its pre-slow rhythm.

Three yeards ahead, Igor Kazov was still lying a close and clever second.

Apple heard a familiar sound from behind. He didn't try to put on more speed. He had no intention of destroying himself. Whatever energy he could save, he would use at the end—if it looked as though he was going to be left too suspiciously far in the van.

Again, as the line of runners ate up the track, the block of British fans appeared. Near it, Apple could see a stationary patch of orange and, far above it, a smaller patch of the same colour that was moving about erratically.

Puzzled, Apple increased slightly the timing of his stride. That kept the pounding from behind at the same volume. The odd sight of the high-jiggling orange patch continued.

Drawing closer, Apple saw that it was the headscarf. It was being waved by June. Obviously, she wanted to ensure his attention. Getting closer still, he stared at her lips.

She mouthed, *"I did not tell about the muggers. I told no one. No one. No one."*

Apple mimed, *"You sure?"*

"Yes, I did not . . ."

He was passing the place now and had to turn his head away. With disinterest he noted that the runner from behind was drawing alongside him. He was telling himself that June could be lying. But there would be no sense in her doing that because he could find out easily enough if she had told of the incident with Green-suit and Coveralls.

Apple ran on. He held the other man marginally behind and on the outside. The bearded runner was four yards ahead. Ten yards beyond that, Igor Kazov was maintaining his close tail on the race leader.

Positioning stayed the same over the following lap.

Apple's chaser was inching up by the time they were nearing the British section. Between flicking glances at the way ahead, Apple kept his eyes on June. She was leaning forward, the scarf stretched between her clenched hands.

When he was close enough to be seen clearly, Apple began on transmitting, *"Watkin told me—"*

He broke off because of the fast, startled look that was shot to him by the man who was almost at his side. Apple realised that he had been shouting. He also realised that this had caused his rival to ease back.

Even though he knew he couldn't be heard above the crowd's boom, Apple yelled again when he mouthed, *"Watkin says he knows of an earlier failing in duty on my part. It can only be the muggers."*

The last word he got out at the final second, before he had to give his vision back to the track.

Apple ran on, still in no discomfort. He held to the same speed as the other man came up again, drew abreast, and, with a frowned warning, began to pull ahead. The warning had been unnecessary; Apple would not have shouted for anything.

During the following lap, his nearest rival ran well clear and the last man started to make himself heard behind. Apple didn't care. He was more interested in what excuse, or lie, or answer June would give on the next passing.

When that occurred, Apple was surprised to see that June

was looking angry. She shook her fists while miming, "*You idiot. That earlier failing was when you chased the bag-snatcher. You ought to have ignored him and gone on to . . .*"

The rendezvous, Apple thought as he ran past. The supposed meeting on Bayswater Road. Man with grey hat in yellow car. Of course, of course, of course. Never let anything interfere with an operation. The deal was yet another prime example of Watkin's double-headed ways, his killing of two birds with one twisted pebble. It had been a test for devotion to duty as well as for running ability.

Apple increased his pace while thinking: So, June didn't tell anyone about Coveralls and Green-suit, who evidently were just common muggers after all. But there was still that other matter.

The footfalls from behind stayed at the same low volume, Apple noted vaguely as he ran on, just as he was inattentive to the registered fact that the other four men were well ahead, strung out except for the leading pair, whose positions were unchanged.

Another lap was covered.

Getting close enough to where June was standing, her eyes intently on his face, Apple worked his lips to form, "*You acted in that scene for me in the park.*"

Frowning, June mouthed, "*What scene?*"

"*When you and some other guy played at Red spies for my listening benefit,*" was all that Apple was able to get out before turning away.

He ran on, keeping up a good speed because he was curious to know what June's reply would be. She, of course, would probably not yet know that he had been told the truth by Watkin. She might not even be there on the next circuit.

But she was, Apple saw, as once more the British section came into view. She was holding both hands on top of her head.

Apple kept to his pace even though he felt like slackening off.

The strain was beginning to tell. But he was still a yard in front of the runner behind.

June looked stricken. Eyes wide, she mimed, *"I did not know it was for you. Watkin did not say that."*

Apple slowed. *"What?"* He dodged his head, annoyed at the interruption, when the trailing runner went by.

June: *"Watkin said it was for the agent who shot the terrorists. For doing that, stepping out of cover, he needed a loyalty test."*

My God, Apple thought as he loped slowly, watching June. That bastard. That putrid bastard Watkin.

June mouthed, *"I would not have done that to you."* She smiled before *"I think you are wonderful."*

Apple: *"Really?"*

June: *"Watch out!"*

Apple switched his head around. Having been running in a straight line instead of curving with the track, he was about to charge smack into the wall. He corrected and looked back again from the other side.

He mouthed, *"Really?"*

"Yes," June sent. She made an urgent pushing motion. *"Run!"*

"Run!" the British fans roared imploringly.

Run! shouted Apple inside his head as he turned away. Run like a maniac!

He ran like a maniac.

Apple charged back to the inside lane. The man who had just passed him was close. Apple quickly caught up. He was level briefly, then going past. He moved to the inner white line.

His feet pounded down on the asphalt. The breeze he created fanned him cool. His body was giving him aches, but in his mind he felt fine. He was exhilarated. He had come back to life.

Apple gained steadily on the next athlete. His progress was matched by an increase in the stadium noise. The crowd was yelling him on: the underdog, the man who comes from behind, the man who tries.

Apple had never tried so hard. At anything. He ran with glaring eyes and bared teeth. He ignored the pain that began in his side.

Gradually Apple came near enough to the man ahead to pull out. He regretted the extra footage needed for that, but told himself to smile. He showed the smile to the athlete as he drew level. It seemed to slow the man down, for Apple found that he was surging ahead.

The yammer of the crowd climbed apace.

Apple went on at a churning, battling grind. He thought in elation: To hell with bastard Watkin. To hell with the service. To hell with crown and country. To hell with duty.

Apple was running for himself. He was running for the individual.

For the last time he came close to the British section. The flags and rattles were going mad. From the corner of his vision Apple saw a leaping, cavorting flash of orange.

The bell sounded.

It meant that the lead runner had entered the final lap. He, Apple saw, was the one who had been in front all the way. Right behind him lay Igor Kazov.

The other two runners were also together, but fighting side by side. They both looked around as they heard the threat of pounding footfalls. Their faces were grim as they turned away again.

Stride by stride, Apple gained on the pair. Once more he regretted having to waste footage by pulling out into another lane, and then another. But once more he told himself to smile.

The pair stayed side by side. With a grin like a snarl, Apple fought his way abreast. Then he battled on past.

He cut to the inside lane. Because of the incredible booming of the crowd, he could no longer hear the sound of his shoes battering the asphalt.

Apple was hurting all over. But the pain seemed to belong to someone else. His rage and elation kept him apart.

Igor Kazov made his move. With half a lap to go, he eased out into the second lane. This he did with style. He angled rather than swerved. He was running smoothly. Igor Kazov was a superbly trained machine.

Deep in his throat, Apple groaned. It was not born of despair, but determination. It was more growl than groan. It helped.

He was catching up to the former leader.

The crowd's racket formed one continuous blare. It seemed impossible that it could rise to an even greater pitch.

That happened, however, as Apple edged up on the man in front of him. He swung out. He smiled. He forged his way abreast. He groaned himself on. He went past.

The noise in the stadium rose to a higher pitch.

Igor Kazov was five yards ahead. Forty yards beyond that lay the finishing line.

Apple knew it was impossible even while telling himself: You can do it, you can do it. You're a maniac.

He made a final, mad effort. In it, all memories of training went out of his mind. He forgot Damian House and Giles Parker. He ran by instinct.

So he did everything wrong.

He allowed his legs to lose their straightness, letting his knees poke up with every stride. It felt like kicking.

He began to wag his head. It suited the rhythmic effort and matched with every other kick.

He drew his hands in and formed them into fists. It felt as though he were punching his way along.

Running badly, madly, Apple ate up the ground. The gap lost its length. Five yards became four, four became three. Igor Kazov glanced back briefly. His second glance back was longer. It showed a face of surprise. When he looked behind a third time, the gap reduced to two yards, his expression was evil with anger.

Apple charged on. He gradually drew out, obliquing into the next lane. There were ten yards to go to the finish. It seemed a thousand miles away.

The crowd was going insane.

Apple came within sweat-flicking reach of Igor. He gained still more on that. He inched along. He went on running like a fool: kicking, punching, wagging his head.

There were five yards to go.

Apple drew alongside the Russian. They were running shoulder to shoulder. Igor shot across a vicious look of warning. Apple gave back his snarled smile.

Two yards to go.

Both men sent their bodies forward into the final, lunging swoop. At this, Igor Kazov was an expert. But Appleton Porter was six feet seven inches tall. His head got there first.

Apple had won.

EPILOGUE

He fell. He fell because there wasn't an ounce of energy left in his body. It would have been impossible for him simply to hold himself upright. So he fell.

Apple hit the asphalt and rolled. The roll was as unplanned and unskillful as the fall. There was no smoothness, no self-protection, in his head-over-tail skittering along the hard ground.

Exterior pain came to join the agony he was now feeling inside: stabs on his hands, elbows, knees, back, skull.

His mind fogged.

It's a nightmare, Apple thought. I'm being attacked outside and in. I must wake up. I've got to escape from the pain and from the screams of these thousands of demons.

Next, he was lying still, on his back. Hands were holding him but he lacked the strength to fight them off. He felt his feet being lifted—and mused that this dream was absurd.

Panic swelled anew in Apple as he now felt something clamp over his nose and mouth. He thought it was a hand; thought he was being smothered. There was nothing he could do. He hadn't even enough energy to scream.

Then clean, sweet, cool air rushed into Apple's lungs and he rose to consciousness. He remembered where he was and what had happened. The clamping object over his lower face, he realised, was an oxygen mask. He smiled as he gulped.

His breathing eased. His lungs slowed their labouring and softened their pain. But the pain elsewhere went on. That he could stand. It was even enjoyable, a proof of his effort and victory.

Apple opened his eyes. He was surrounded by anxious faces. He found the strength to raise one hand, push the oxygen mask away. To the faces he said feebly, in French, "I'm all right. Thank you. Let me get up, please."

He couldn't have managed it alone. The hands lifted him to his feet. He stood swaying. The faces were still all around him, but he could see above them easily.

The stadium was still a bedlam of noise—shouting voices, rattles, and the nasal drone of the loudspeakers. The stands were a swarm of writhing movement.

Hands in the small of his back, gasping, Apple looked back toward the British section. It was a mass of waving flags. Nearby, June was trying to climb down the wall.

Apple looked at his immediate area. Among the recovering athletes, he saw Igor Kazov. The Russian was breathing heavily. He met Apple's gaze with a baleful glare. That heavy breathing wasn't totally due to physical effort.

Weakly, Apple pushed his way through the people around him. He tottered over to Igor. Offering his hand, he gasped in Russian, "The rest of the formula."

Igor Kazov ignored the hand. His simian face twitching, he told Apple to go and have sexual intercourse with a lame pig. He added, "You get nothing from me."

Apple told Igor that he could go and have carnal knowledge

of a cross-eyed bear. He added, "No, an ape. You'd be well matched."

Surprise joined the rage in the runner's face.

Apple looked along the track. June was hanging midway down the wall, but being ordered back by a policeman.

"Listen, idiot," Apple said, turning to Igor. "I'm not in the espionage business. I work for neither British Intelligence nor the CIA. Do you think a bean-pole like me could ever be a spy? If you do, you're even more stupid than you look."

As Igor blinked, Apple glanced the other way. June was using the policeman to help herself down.

Igor Kazov said, "I don't understand."

Apple told him, "I simply happen to be a runner who can speak Russian. So I was hired for this job. I'm doing it strictly for the cash. Half down and the other half on delivery of info. Get me?"

Igor nodded warily. "Yes."

"I don't care about any other info after this. It's only today's I want. And I'm going to get it. If I don't, I'll report you to the KGB."

Igor's jaw dropped. His face took on a look of terror.

"I mean it," Apple said. "I need that cash. So start giving."

Slowly at first, then faster as he glanced worriedly all around him, the Russian began to talk.

While absorbing, Apple looked along the track. With part of his mind he registered that June was down on the ground and trying to pull free of the policeman.

Igor Kazov finished. "That's all," he whispered before turning quickly and moving away.

Apple wondered if he would retain all the numbers and letters. He knew he would. He was showing off for himself. But the wonder gave him an idea.

As he went into a wobbly walk back along the track, Apple

thought of what he could do. He would tell Angus Watkin that bits here and there among the sequences were eluding him. To bring them to mind he would need a holiday. To make the holiday the restful success it needed to be, he would have to have the company of June, who could help jog his memory. Both Upstairs and the CIA would have to play along.

A month, Apple decided, noting that June had wrenched free of the policeman and was running forward. A month in the West Indies. Palm trees and beaches. And the company of someone who thought he was wonderful.

Apple wobbled on to meet June, laughing weakly.

Marc Lovell is the author of two previous Appleton Porter novels, *The Spy with His Head in the Clouds* and *The Spy Game,* as well as many others, including *Hand over Mind* and *A Voice from the Living.* Mr. Lovell has lived on the island of Majorca for the last twenty years.